·· ᵇᵧ date shown.

TORCHWOOD
CONSEQUENCES

Recent titles in the *Torchwood* series from BBC Books:

TORCHWOOD
CONSEQUENCES

James Moran
Joseph Lidster
Andrew Cartmel
Sarah Pinborough
David Llewellyn

2 4 6 8 10 9 7 5 3 1

Published in 2009 by BBC Books, an imprint of Ebury Publishing
A Random House Group company

© David Llewellyn, Sarah Pinborough, Andrew Cartmel, James Moran and
Joseph Lidster, 2009
The authors have asserted their right to be identified as the authors of this
Work in accordance with the Copyright, Design and Patents Act 1988.

Torchwood is a BBC Wales production for BBC One
Executive Producers: Russell T Davies and Julie Gardner

Original series created by Russell T Davies and broadcast on BBC Television.
'Torchwood' and the Torchwood logo are trademarks of the
British Broadcasting Corporation and are used under licence.

The Random House Group Limited Reg. No. 954009.
Addresses for companies within the Random House Group can be found at
www.randomhouse.co.uk

A CIP catalogue record for this book is available from the British Library.

ISBN 978 1 846 07784 5

The Random House Group Limited supports The Forest Stewardship Council
(FSC), the leading international forest certification organisation.
All our titles that are printed on Greenpeace approved FSC certified paper
carry the FSC logo. Our paper procurement policy can be found at
www.rbooks.co.uk/environment

Commissioning Editor: Albert DePetrillo
Series Editor: Steve Tribe
Production Controller: Phil Spencer

Cover design by Lee Binding @ Tea Lady © BBC 2009
Typeset in Albertina and Century Gothic
Printed and bound in Germany by GGP Media GmbH

Contents

The Baby Farmers

DAVID LLEWELLYN

Through driving rain and howling wind she walked, the shawl barely covering her head and shoulders, let alone the baby in her arms. The skies above the town were lit up with incandescent flashes of lightning, followed soon after by percussive drum rolls of thunder, each sounding for all the world like a monstrous funeral march. And yet the baby slept.

The young woman, Mary, passed the jeering patrons of the Vulcan Hotel and walked beneath the railway bridge, trudging her way through deep, dark puddles before she reached the meeting place on the banks of the canal.

They were already waiting for her: the black carriage drawn by a pair of stout black horses, the coach driver hidden from view by a thick scarf and the brim of a misshapen stovepipe hat. As Mary drew near, the carriage door opened and an older woman, matronly and severe, her face pinched and without make-up, stepped out.

'Mrs Thomas?' she asked, unfolding an umbrella to shield herself from the pouring rain.

Mary nodded, and curtsied.

'I'm Mrs Blight,' said the older woman. She gestured towards the bundle in Mary's arms. 'And that is the child?'

The younger woman nodded sheepishly.

'And *Mr* Thomas?' asked Mrs Blight.

'He doesn't know,' said Mary. 'He's in Natal. With the army. He's been there a year now.'

Mrs Blight nodded with a vague air of disdain. 'I see,' she said curtly.

Mary unfolded the shawl a little so that Mrs Blight could see the baby.

'And it's a boy?' asked Mrs Blight.

Mary nodded. There were tears in her eyes. 'You've found a home for him?' she asked.

'Yes,' said Mrs Blight, without a trace of warmth. 'A very wealthy couple. The husband is in shipping. They've wanted a son for many years but have not been blessed. He'll go to a loving home, you have my word.'

Mary nodded once more, and looked down at her infant son, bowing her head and trying her best not to cry. 'His name is Michael,' she sobbed, wiping her eyes with a handkerchief.

'His *name* shall be chosen by his *parents*,' said Mrs Blight coldly. 'And now the issue of our fee?'

'Of course.' Mary reached into her purse, taking out a handful of coins and handing them to Mrs Blight. 'It's all I have.'

Mrs Blight inspected the money, flaring her nostrils. 'It'll do,' she said. 'Though Lord knows, for any less I'd have sent you to the workhouse on Cowbridge Road and told you to keep it.'

'Thank you,' said Mary. Closing her eyes to fight back further tears, she kissed the baby just once on the forehead, stirring him from his slumber, before passing him to Mrs Blight.

Cradling the baby in one arm, Mrs Blight nodded. 'Good night, Mrs Thomas,' she said, climbing the steps into the carriage, and closing the door behind her with a loud clunk.

With a crack of his whip, the coach driver turned the carriage, the hooves of the horses clopping and sploshing along the waterlogged street, and they drove off into the night.

Mindless of the rain and the puddles, Mary fell to her knees and wept. She would never see her baby again.

It was all wonderfully gothic, she had decided. The flashes of lightning, the rumbling of thunder, and the ruins of the old house. Rather like a scene by one of the Brontës. Of course, it was hard for Emily Holroyd to imagine the eponymous heroine of *Jane Eyre* climbing over a wrought-iron fence after nightfall, and all but impossible to picture *Wuthering Heights'* Cathy searching for unimaginable monsters and fantastical creatures in the dim glow of a zinc-carbon powered flashlight.

Still, as much as Emily searched, no such creatures or monsters could be found. The grounds of Herbert House, an abandoned edifice on the edges of Crockherbtown, were filled with ferns and ivy and unkempt trees, but little else.

What, then, could have caused Torchwood's instruments to act so very strangely? Everything about the data collected back at the Hub suggested that the Rift had once again opened, and that something had come through. Emily would take no chances; in one hand she held the torch, the light from which grew fainter by the minute, while in the other she grasped her revolver.

When she had been exploring the ruins for almost an hour, and was close to giving up the search altogether, she came across something quite unexpected.

There, nestled between the tangled, thorny nest of a rosebush and the walls of the old house, was a book. Had the book been there for any length of time, in this weather, she might have expected its pages to be drenched and sodden. Instead, the book was in pristine condition, as if it had been left there only moments ago.

Emily lifted the book, careful not to catch herself or the sleeves of her overcoat on the thorns, and opened it. A small sheet of paper fluttered to the ground, and she bent down to retrieve it.

'Dear Lord,' she whispered, as she started to read. 'I…'

But try as she might, there was nothing more to say. She was speechless.

Jack Harkness opened the office door, striding out into the Hub, and Alice Guppy followed.

'Jack… Stop right this instant. That's an order,' she said.

Jack turned on his heels. 'You forget,' he said, grinning, 'I'm freelance. I don't take orders.'

'More the reason to wait until Emily returns,' said Alice. 'That telegram is addressed to *her*.'

'And she's not here,' said Jack. 'So I'll go.'

Sitting at his desk, flicking through the pages of a dossier, Charles Gaskell looked up at them and sighed.

'What's the matter?' he asked. 'Is our pet freak misbehaving again?'

'Pet *freak*?' said Jack, in a tone of mild outrage. 'Who're you calling a pet *freak*?'

Gaskell raised an eyebrow, and then turned once more to Alice.

'We've received a telegram,' she explained, 'addressed to *Emily*. From some journalist at the *Western Mail*. William something-or-other.'

'Mayhew,' Jack told her. 'William Mayhew. He wants to meet Emily at the Coliseum Music Hall in Butetown at 9 p.m. *Tonight*.'

'And *you're* going?' asked Gaskell.

Jack nodded.

'I'm not sure Miss Holroyd will be happy about that,' Gaskell mused. 'If it's addressed to *her*, I mean.'

'But she's not here,' said Jack, 'and I am. And I don't see anyone else volunteering to go.'

Gaskell inspected his pocket watch and turned to Alice. 'It's almost a quarter to the hour,' he said, and then to Jack: 'What does the telegram say, anyhow?'

Jack unfolded the piece of paper and read from it.

'Please meet at Coliseum Theatre, Butetown, 9 p.m. I shall be wearing white carnation. Balcony row F. Important information re: HMS Hades. Urgent.'

Gaskell sighed. 'Let him go,' he said. 'Anyway... Gentleman wearing a white carnation sounds much more like Jack's kind of liaison than yours or Miss Holroyd's, if you catch my drift.'

Alice rolled her eyes and shook her head.

Jack turned to Gaskell, smiling. 'Sure you don't want to come along?' he said with a wink.

Gaskell folded his arms, leaning back in his chair, and shook his head. 'No, thank you, Harkness,' he said. 'I'm not really a fan of musical theatre.'

'Sure about that?' asked Jack.

'Yes, Jack,' Gaskell replied, wearily. 'No matter how hard you try to convince me otherwise.'

Holding an oil lamp in one hand and fumbling with his keys in the other, Mr Crank, the night porter at the University College, muttered under his breath.

'What sort of an hour do they call this?' he grumbled. 'It's blowin' a gale and raining cats and dogs and still there's somebody knockin' at the blimmin' door.'

When he'd finally found the key and unlocked the large wooden door, he was surprised to see, standing on the library steps, a smartly dressed woman carrying a large leather-bound book. She was soaked through from the rain but showed little sign of being in any way distressed, as Mr Crank might have imagined a woman should be, stuck in the rain on her own.

'Can... can I help you?' he asked, holding up the lamp to

get a better look at her.

'You must let me in,' replied the woman. 'My name is Emily Holroyd. I am here on a matter of the utmost urgency, in the name of Her Majesty's Government.'

Crank chuckled softly to himself. 'You don't say?' he laughed. 'What is it? Chinese invading, are they? Or maybe the French?'

The young woman shook her head dismissively and pushed her way past Mr Crank.

'Look here,' said the old man, flustered. 'Did I say you could come in?'

She wasn't listening to him. Instead she was making her way through the labyrinthine walkways of the library, lighting her way with what looked like one of the new-style electrical torches. Mr Crank tried his best to follow, but she was too quick for him.

'Hang on a minute, Miss,' he said. 'This is University property. If the Dean finds out about this, he'll have my guts for garters…'

It was too late. He'd lost her. The ground floor of the library was vast, with too many dark and unknowable corners at this hour of the night. She could be anywhere. His heart began to race, and he found himself short of breath. What if she was a thief? There were volumes in the library worth a small fortune. He could wave goodbye to his pension, that was for sure, not to mention the chances of finding another job anywhere within fifty miles of Cardiff. As panic began to set in, Mr Crank the night porter was startled by the woman's voice.

'There,' she said, appearing at his side and smiling sweetly. 'All done.'

Mr Crank now noticed that she was no longer carrying the book. Before he could ask her what she had done with it, the woman nodded graciously.

'Thank you so much,' she said, walking out into the rain. 'Good evening.'

And with that, she was gone.

With her face painted white and her cheeks daubed with circles of bright pink, the young woman made her way towards the centre of the stage, a parasol perched daintily on her shoulder. To one side of the stage, the piano player, a Chinese gent in a bowler hat and waistcoat, played the opening chords before she sang:

> *I'm a young girl, and have just come over,*
> *Over from the country where they do things big,*
> *And amongst the boys I've got a lover,*
> *And since I've got a lover, why I don't care a fig…*

Jack Harkness edged his way through the gloom, down the wooden steps of the balcony until he came to row F. Standing at its edge he saw, in the faint light reflected from the stage, a portly middle-aged man with a white carnation pinned to his lapel. Much to the chagrin of those already seated, Jack shuffled past them and sat down next to him.

'Hi,' he said, holding out a hand. 'I'm not Emily Holroyd.'

'I should say not,' said the man with the carnation. 'May I ask who you *are*?'

'Jack Harkness,' said Jack, shaking his hand. 'And you're Mayhew?'

Mayhew nodded.

On stage, the singer gestured toward the balcony with one open hand.

The boy I love is up in the gallery,
The boy I love is looking now at me,
There he is, can't you see, waving his handkerchief,
As merry as a robin that sings on a tree.

Jack smiled down at the stage, and then turned once more to Mayhew.

'D'you think she's talking about me?' he asked. 'Only I forgot my handkerchief.'

Mayhew huffed. 'Should I assume that you are affiliated with Torchwood?' he asked, sternly.

Gauging the seriousness of his tone, Jack stopped smiling and nodded.

'Yes,' he said. 'You should. But what's with the meeting place? It's not exactly where I'd expect to find a well-heeled gent such as yourself. They've got *Pirates Of Penzance* at the Philharmonic.'

'That's exactly the point,' said Mayhew. 'Nobody would expect to find me here. Besides which, I can't *stand* Gilbert and Sullivan.'

Jack laughed. 'Each to his own,' he said, and then, after a pause, 'So what is it you know about HMS *Hades*?'

Mayhew said nothing at first, toying with the ends of his grey moustache with forefinger and thumb before answering.

'We shouldn't talk here,' he said. 'This was just to make sure I could trust you.'

'And do you?'

Mayhew looked at Jack with one eyebrow arched. 'You'll do,' he said.

Together they stood and made their way slowly out of the darkened auditorium, just as the song came to an end and the audience began cheering raucously, waving their tankards of beer (complimentary with their ticket for less than a shilling) above their heads.

As Jack and Mayhew stepped out into the rain-slicked and windswept street, they found it near deserted.

'Not a carriage to be seen,' said Mayhew. 'How typical. That's the only trouble with frequenting these parts of town. Not many coach drivers will come down here after dark, especially not in this weather. Come along… We may have better luck nearer the Square…'

They turned a corner, from the lamplight of Bute Street into one of the darker side streets, making their way towards Mount Stuart Square. Jack placed little stock in the notion of extrasensory perception, or at least in his *own*, but still he felt uneasy. Something wasn't right.

His fears were confirmed by the clattering of horse's hooves and the rattling of carriage wheels against the cobbled street. He had little chance to react.

As he turned on his heels, he saw the carriage and the silhouettes of men with guns. He heard the crack of gunshots and saw the bright flash of muzzle flares, one after the other. He felt the all-too-familiar warmth of hot lead passing through his flesh and the warm-but-wet trickle of blood on his skin. Falling to the ground, his vision blurring and the sounds around him fading away as echoes, he saw Mayhew fall beside him, a gaping bloody hole where his left eye should have been.

'And you let him go?' Emily was almost shouting.

Alice could barely look her in the eye, her cheeks burning with embarrassment.

'Actually,' said Gaskell, 'Miss Guppy didn't want to. She tried to stop him. I suggested it would be the best idea.'

Emily turned to him and shook her head.

'Mr Gaskell, *really*,' she said. 'I expected better of you. Captain Harkness remains an unknown quantity. We understand him little more than we understand those *things* that come through the Rift, and yet you have sent him out there in my stead?'

'I'm sorry,' replied Gaskell. 'But you weren't here. We didn't know where you were.'

'As I said,' snapped Emily, 'I was investigating possible activity in Crockherbtown.'

'And was there any?' asked Alice. 'Activity, I mean?'

Emily shook her head. 'No,' she replied. 'I found nothing.'

She paused, taking a deep breath, and composed herself.

'Now,' she continued, 'I think we should wait until morning.'

'Morning?' said Gaskell. 'Really? But Harkness *still* hasn't returned.'

'No,' said Emily. 'But William Mayhew is just another

19

eccentric with a taste for the obscure. It wouldn't surprise me if their little rendezvous results in nothing more alarming than the discovery of some sideshow exhibit. A bearded lady, perhaps, or the nightmarish work of some deranged taxidermist, stitching together monkeys and fish and calling them mermaids. There's little we can achieve by sitting here and worrying all night.'

Gaskell laughed, rising from his desk and putting on his bowler hat. 'In which case, ladies,' he said, as he made his way across the Hub, 'I'll take my leave. There's a shot of rum and a lovely barmaid waiting for me at the Six Bells. Goodnight, both.'

As he left, closing the door behind him, Alice turned to Emily. 'Are you still angry with me?' she asked, a little timidly.

Emily thought this over for a moment before smiling. 'Not really,' she replied, gently brushing Alice's cheek with one finger. 'Just tired. Come along, Miss Guppy. Time for bed.'

By sunrise the clouds had dispersed, leaving only a thin layer of fog over the mudflats of the bay and the ramshackle streets of Butetown.

Gaskell made his way past the Norwegian Church and carried on until he reached the very edge of the docks. Descending a narrow flight of steps, he walked along the quayside until he came to an anonymous wooden door. It was covered, from top to bottom, in yellowing posters advertising past events: Buffalo Bill's Wild West show at Sophia Gardens, the Maritime Exhibition of '96, and Mr

Charles Dickens' reading at the Taliesin Lodge some thirty Christmases past.

Checking there was nobody around to see him, Gaskell unlocked the door, and stepped inside.

Moments later he walked into the Hub to find that Alice and Emily were already sitting at their desks, waiting for him.

'What time do you call this?' asked Emily, rising from her chair and holding up her pocket watch for dramatic effect.

'I know,' groaned Gaskell, 'and you have my sincerest apologies…'

'Ah,' said Alice, smiling. 'Methinks our Romeo hath not been in bed tonight.'

Gaskell shot her a glare of mock annoyance, and then winked, his mouth curling into a smile.

'Well,' said Emily, interrupting the moment. 'I'm sure we'll hear all the *ghastly* details at a later date. Captain Harkness still hasn't returned.'

Gaskell took off his hat, his expression suddenly grave. 'He hasn't?'

'No. And all attempts to contact William Mayhew have proven quite fruitless. In light of Captain Harkness's disappearance, we are going to investigate the matter further. HMS *Hades*…'

Gaskell nodded.

'What do you know of it?'

'Not much,' he replied. 'Used to be a 42-gun frigate. It was one of the ships that accompanied Napoleon to St Helena in 1815. Decommissioned in 1869.'

'Well,' said Emily. 'That's rather more than "not much", Mr Gaskell.'

'Yes, well,' said Gaskell. 'Old naval trivia. They drum it into you.'

'Of course. Does the name Sir Henry Montague mean anything to you?'

Gaskell paused for a moment, sitting on the edge of his desk. His head still throbbed and his mouth was dry, but now was not the time to feel sorry for oneself.

'*Admiral* Sir Henry Montague?' he asked, eventually.

'The same.'

'He's well thought of, ma'am. One of the most respected naval leaders since Nelson. I met him when we were anchored at Portsmouth. He came to inspect the ship. He lives just outside Cardiff these days. But how does *he* fit into all this?'

Emily lifted a document from her desk and, reading from it, made her way across the Hub.

'Admiral Sir Henry Montague,' she began, 'bought HMS *Hades* from the Navy shortly after it was decommissioned. It was brought from Plymouth to Cardiff and converted into a ragged school for wayward boys and orphans, under the management of Tiberius Finch and Mrs Gertrude Blight, often referred to as the Widow Blight.'

'Sounds delightful.'

'Finch is a local philanthropist. Studied as a surgeon at the Royal College Of Medicine, but failed to graduate following some kind of scandal in his final year. Blight is something of an enigma, I'm afraid. Hard to find out much about her, except that she's a widow.'

'So our plan…?'

Now Alice stepped forward. 'Well,' she said, with an almost coquettish smile, 'seeing as you're an old friend of Montague's, we thought you might like to pay him a visit?'

'And what about you two?'

'We're going to *Hades*,' said Emily. 'In a manner of speaking.'

It was difficult, if not impossible, for Alice to imagine HMS *Hades* ever being a warship. Stripped of its masts and sails, its cannons long gone and its hatches transformed into soot-covered windows, the *Hades* sat with its hull half-buried in the muddy east bank of the river. Where once there had been decks there were now cobbled-together shacks, like mismatched houses, running from one end of the ship to the other, making the place look more like some disastrously constructed version of Noah's Ark than a majestic frigate that had once escorted Napoleon to his exile.

From its decaying rooftops crooked chimneys belched out thick, acrid clouds of black smoke, but there were few other signs that anyone might be onboard.

'And they call it a *ragged* school?' asked Alice, as they stepped onto the ramp leading to the ship's only entrance.

'Yes,' replied Emily. 'A school for destitute and homeless boys – orphans, urchins…'

Alice paused before the large and windowless wooden door, in the centre of which was a fearsome wrought-iron knocker cast in the shape of Cerberus' three heads.

'Just think,' she said. 'If I'd been born a boy I might have ended up here.'

Emily turned to her, as if surprised by the statement, but then nodded sympathetically.

'Yes,' she said softly, 'I suppose you might have.'

She reached forward and slammed the knocker three times. They waited for an age, standing on the wooden ramp, listening to the sounds of clanking and hissing machinery in the belly of the ship. Eventually the wooden door opened, and they were greeted by a short, stout woman dressed in black.

'Can I help you?' asked the woman.

Emily extended her gloved hand.

'We are from the Torchwood Institute,' she said. 'I was wondering whether we might speak with the proprietor of this establishment?'

The woman looked from Emily to Alice with an expression of disdain, and then back again. She shook Emily's hand very briefly.

'I am the proprie*tress* of this establishment,' she told them. 'My name is Mrs Blight. How may I be of service?'

'We were hoping to visit the ragged school,' Emily continued. 'Our work includes local philanthropy in and around Cardiff, and we have heard so much about your good work here…'

'I am afraid that will not be possible,' snapped Mrs Blight, coldly. 'We do not permit female visitors to the school. As I'm sure you will appreciate, our wards are all boys, some of them approaching maturity. It could prove most disruptive if two young women such as yourselves were to enter their place of learning.'

Emily narrowed her eyes, scrutinising Mrs Blight very carefully, not caring if the older woman realised it.

'I see,' she said, at last. 'Of course. Well perhaps you could pass our best wishes on to Mr Finch. Good day, Mrs Blight.'

'Good day, Miss Holroyd. Miss Guppy.'

Nodding politely to them both, Mrs Blight closed the door, and both Emily and Alice heard the sound of several bolts being slid into place on the other side.

'Curiouser and curiouser…' said Alice, as she and Emily made their way back down the ramp.

The grandfather clock chimed eleven, and in its ornate cage a zebra finch fluttered from its perch. Gaskell waited in the hall outside the Admiral's study, sat on a wooden chair. The tiled floor before him was lit up in a kaleidoscope of colours, projected from a distant stained glass window. From the study he heard the voice of Montague's butler, Mr Phillips.

'Sir, there is a gentleman here to see you…'

'Yes, Phillips? Who is he?'

'A *coloured* gentleman, sir.'

There was a long pause. Gaskell smiled to himself and tried not to chuckle.

'Really?' said Montague. 'Is he looking for *work?*'

'No, sir. He says he's from the Torchwood institute, and that he would like to speak to you.'

Another long pause.

'I see. Well you'd better show him in.'

Seconds later Phillips emerged from the study.

'Mr Gaskell, if you would care to follow me.'

Gaskell rose from the chair and followed the butler into Montague's study. Two of the study's walls were lined, from floor to ceiling, with book shelves. A third was decorated with boiseries on which were hung paintings of naval battles. The Admiral's desk was situated before a vast bay window, beyond which there lay the fields above Penarth's headland and, further on, the sea.

Admiral Sir Henry Montague was a tall, lean gentleman, dressed in a tweed three-piece suit, his hair a silvering mixture of grey and black. He smiled warmly as he stepped out from behind his desk.

'Mr Charles Gaskell,' Phillips announced.

Montague approached Gaskell and shook his hand.

'Mr Gaskell,' he said. 'How do you do? Please, take a seat. Would you care for tea, or coffee, perhaps?'

Gaskell politely declined the offer, and Montague dismissed his butler. As Montague returned to his chair, Gaskell looked around the study. He had never imagined he would find himself there, in the home of Sir Henry Montague, being asked if he'd care for tea or coffee. It took some effort just to mask his excitement.

'So,' said Montague, 'Mr Gaskell… How may I help you?'

'Well first of all,' said Gaskell, smiling, 'I'd just like to say what an honour it is to meet you again, sir.'

'Again?' queried Montague. 'I'm sorry, my dear fellow, but have we met before?'

'Yes,' said Gaskell. 'HMS *Atropos*. We were anchored in Portsmouth. You came aboard to inspect the ship, sir.'

Montague smiled. 'Ah… You're an old sea dog, then?'

Gaskell nodded.

'Well why didn't you say?' Montague bellowed. 'I'd have offered you something stronger than tea or coffee! So you say you're with the Torchwood Institute?'

'Yes, sir.'

'Hmm. Can't say I know much about that. It all sounds very clandestine. Not sure how I can be of service, though…'

'Well, sir, as it happens we're making enquiries about the *Hades*, sir.'

Montague's smile faded a little and his eyes narrowed. 'HMS *Hades*,' he said, drumming his fingers on the desk. 'Well… Of course, I am the owner of the ship. My name is on the deeds. As for the day-to-day running of the place, I have little involvement. I visit them once every few months, see how the boys are doing. You know, they're all so very cheerful, aren't they? The poor, I mean.'

'Quite,' said Gaskell. 'But we have received a rather alarming telegram from a local journalist by the name of Mayhew. He claims to have important information regarding the *Hades*.'

'Important information?' Montague blustered. 'Mayhew, you say? Hmph… Think I've heard of the chap. What kind of important information does he claim to have?'

'We're not exactly sure, sir. It appears he may have gone missing.'

Montague leaned back in his chair and folded his arms, laughing softly. 'I see,' he said. 'Well, if you ask me, this Mayhew sounds like just another provincial hack with too much time on his hands. That's the trouble in peacetime, you see? Not enough news to cover, so fellows like him go around concocting plots and sinister motives from nothing.'

'Well, sir, Mayhew hasn't mentioned anything about a plot, or—'

'Give him enough time and he will do.'

'As I said, sir… He may be missing.'

Montague shook his head and huffed. 'Typical journalist,' he said. 'Probably sleeping off a surfeit of gin on the floor of some tavern, just you mark my words.'

Gaskell laughed, and Montague smiled for the first time in an age.

'You can have my word on the matter,' Montague continued. 'There is nothing sinister going on aboard the *Hades*. Mr Finch and Mrs Blight do sterling work with the boys there. It speaks volumes of this dismal age that some would cast suspicions and doubts upon their charitable endeavours. Now, Mr Gaskell, unless there is anything more that I can help you with…?'

'Not at all,' said Gaskell, rising from his chair and shaking Montague by the hand. 'You've been most helpful.'

Deep in the belly of HMS *Hades*, in a room without windows, Tiberius Finch gazed down into his microscope at a cluster of cells and smiled approvingly.

Finch was a tall man of generous proportions, his unruly grey hair tamed into a short ponytail, and his face adorned with a fine beard and moustache. His face, or what could be seen of it above the beard, was blemished by a network of ruptured capillaries, the result of his fondness for whisky, giving him a perennially ruddy complexion.

He was surrounded, in this darkened room, by mementos from his days studying medicine – volume after volume of medical journals and textbooks, framed anatomical diagrams and models rendered in wax. Each model resembled nothing so much as the work of a butcher or a madman: the severed human head on a bureau in the far corner, its hideously lifelike skin peeled away revealing the glistening orb of an eyeball, the cheekbone, and the muscles of the jaw; or the section of a woman's abdomen rent open to reveal a tiny, perfectly detailed waxwork foetus. Each ghastly object was illuminated by little more than the flickering of the oil lamp on Finch's desk.

His concentration was interrupted very suddenly by a knock at the door.

'Come in,' he growled.

The door opened, and Mrs Blight entered the room.

'Mr Finch, sir,' she said, her features gaunt and stark in the lamplight. 'We've had visitors.'

Finch rose from behind the desk, his head very nearly touching the ceiling. 'Visitors?' he said. 'What sort of visitors?'

'Torchwood.'

Finch huffed and then smiled, his lips curling back to reveal yellowing teeth. 'Looking for their friend, were they?'

'Perhaps.'

Finch walked around his desk, picking up a small vial that was placed next to the microscope. He held it against the lamplight, sloshing its liquid red contents against the glass.

'And did they suspect anything?'

'Hard to say,' said Mrs Blight. 'But it's only a matter of time. What if they return?'

'You may be right,' said Finch, turning to her and smiling with menace. 'They may return. And we shall be waiting for them.'

As Mrs Blight nodded, closing the door behind her, Finch returned the vial to his desk. On its side there was a label, and written on that label, in black ink, the words:

PATIENT 237 - HARKNESS, J.

Peter ran across the marshlands, and Sam followed after him.

'Keep up!' Peter yelled, waving the broken branch above his head as if it were a sabre. 'I can seem 'em! Thousands of 'em!'

Sam stopped running and braced himself against his knees, gasping for breath. He could feel the water soaking into his brand new shoes. His mother was going to give him a clip around the ear when he got home.

'What are you *doing*?' cried Peter, turning around, still brandishing the stick. 'I can see Zulus! They're down in the gorge!'

'I'm *tired*,' Sam wheezed. 'When do *I* get to be Chard?'

'You're Bromhead,' said Peter, as if offended. 'Bromhead won a VC too, you know.'

'I *know*, but *I* want to be Chard. And besides… There was no gorge at Rorke's Drift. We're doing this all wrong…'

'Stop whining!' shouted Peter. 'There's Zulus in the gorge…'

Before Sam could offer any further protest, Peter had turned and begun charging once more, bellowing at the top of his voice. Sam shook his head and rolled his eyes.

Peter was always getting him into trouble. Sam's mother had given him strict instructions that he was to come straight home from school – no dawdling and certainly no mucking about on the marshes. It had been Peter's idea to come home this way, and now here they were, up to their ankles in water and fighting imaginary tribesmen on an imaginary veldt.

At least, Sam supposed, they were running in the right direction. He could already see the rooftops of his street and the chapel graveyard. If he followed Peter towards his non-existent gorge he would eventually get home, even if it was a little later than his mother would have liked.

He had been running for no more than a minute when, a little way ahead of him, Peter fell out of view, vanishing behind the reeds. Sam stopped running.

'Peter?' he called out. 'Peter? What's happened?'

His friend did not reply.

'Peter!' he shouted. 'Stop messing about!'

After another moment's pause, the only sound that of the seagulls swooping and diving overhead, Sam began to run once more. He sloshed through the water, regardless of how drenched his new shoes might get, until he came at last to where Peter had fallen.

He found his friend sat on the ground hugging his knees to his chest, his face gaunt with terror.

'What is it?' Sam asked. 'Why did you fall?'

Peter looked up at him, startled, and with his hand shaking uncontrollably he pointed at something lying half-buried in the water and the mud.

It was a severed arm.

'And you believed him?' asked Alice as she followed Gaskell across the Hub.

'Yes,' said Gaskell. 'Why shouldn't I? The man is an *Admiral*, Alice, or does that mean nothing to you?'

'Not particularly,' Alice replied. 'But then I wasn't in the Navy.'

'Sir Henry Montague is a great man,' Gaskell continued. 'And I don't think we'll get very far if we start throwing wild accusations at him.'

He strode over to the entrance to Emily's office.

'Ma'am,' he said, 'I've spoken to Montague…'

'So I heard,' said Emily, looking up from a document. '*All* of it.'

Alice appeared at Gaskell's side.

'Anyway,' Emily continued, 'if the two of you are done arguing, I think I may have found something rather interesting.'

They entered the office and stood before her desk. Emily turned the document so that they could read it.

'What is it?' Gaskell asked.

'Records,' replied Emily. 'Students who have graduated from the Hades Ragged School since 1889.'

'And…?'

Emily turned the document once more and held it alongside an open dossier.

'This name here,' she replied. 'Benjamin K. Flambard. Born on the Third of August 1883, graduated in July 1895.'

'So?' said Gaskell. 'Doesn't sound particularly odd to me.'

'No,' Emily told him. 'Unless one considers that a Benjamin K. Flambard, born on the Third of August 1883 *died* at St Helen's Hospital. On the *Fourth* of August that same year.'

'When he was a day old…?'

'Exactly.'

The office fell into silence.

Gaskell leaned against the desk and raised a hand to his mouth. 'You mean to say that *all* these names… *all* the boys who graduated… They're all the names of babies who died shortly after birth?'

'Not all,' said Emily. 'But I've been able to match more than thirty so far.'

'Good grief,' gasped Alice. 'They're taking the names of dead babies and falsifying the records…'

Emily nodded.

'But if they aren't *teaching* boys there, what *are* they doing?'

'There's more,' said Emily, taking a copy of a newspaper from a drawer and opening it next to the documents. 'These are the classified advertisements for the *Western Mail*. See here… "*Wealthy couple wish to adopt child, preferably newborn. Fee negotiable.*"'

'Fee?' said Gaskell. 'You mean they expect to be *paid* to adopt someone's baby?'

'Baby farming,' Alice said, her voice barely louder than a whisper. 'Desperate women without the means to look after their child pay a small fee to have the child taken off them. But what has this got to do with the *Hades*?'

Emily pointed at a number below the advertisement.

'*That*,' she said, 'is a telephone number. Now there are not a great many telephones in Cardiff, but that one just happens to be listed at a property in Butetown.'

'The *Hades*?' asked Gaskell.

Emily laughed. 'Oh no,' she said. 'They haven't made it *that* easy for us. The property in question happens to be empty. A house belonging to a Mr Edmund Blight.'

Alice smiled knowingly. 'Don't tell me,' she said. 'Late husband of…'

'Exactly. It appears our missing friend Mayhew may have stumbled upon this rather interesting clue—'

Before Emily could say another word, she was interrupted by the ringing of the telephone. She lifted the receiver to her ear.

'Cardiff one-six-five?' she said.

There was a long pause.

'I see. Of course. You have been most helpful, as always. Thank you, and good day.'

Emily returned the receiver to its cradle and let out a long sigh.

'What is it?' asked Alice.

'Unfortunate news,' replied Emily. 'It would appear that our missing friend Mayhew has been found. In *several* locations.'

Gaskell grimaced, covering his mouth with his hand. Alice sighed and shook her head.

'And Harkness?' she asked.

'No news of him, I'm afraid.'

'So what do we do now?'

'We wait,' said Emily. 'Until nightfall. And then we pay another visit to HMS *Hades*.'

'Penny for your thoughts?'

Gaskell looked up from his glass of rum, saw Clara and smiled. 'Not sure they're worth that much,' he said.

The smoking room of the Six Bells was almost empty. Gaskell sat at the bar, while in the far corner an old retired sailor in a peaked cap sat puffing away on his pipe and nursing a pewter tankard of beer. The only other person in the room was Clara, the barmaid, a towel resting on one shoulder and her blonde hair tied up in a bun.

Clara was 26 years old, with eyes the colour of tropical seas, her beauty marred only by a puckered line of scar tissue, no more than two inches in length, on the side of her throat. Although it was only noticeable in a certain light, Gaskell knew she was still conscious of it every waking moment of the day.

'You look like you've the weight of the world on your shoulders,' Clara said, leaning on the bar so that her face was now only inches from his.

'Do I?' asked Gaskell.

Clara nodded sympathetically. 'Don't suppose you'd ever tell me what it is, though,' she said. ''Nother rum?'

Gaskell shook his head. 'No,' he said. 'Not while I'm on duty.'

Clara laughed. 'You know something, Charlie?' she said. 'One of these days you'll tell me what it is you do for a living.'

'Oh, I doubt that,' said Gaskell, winking at the beautiful young barmaid.

As he drained the last drops of rum from his glass and felt its warmth trickle down his throat and onto his chest, the door opened. Reflected in the mirror behind the bar, he saw two men enter. They stood behind him, and one of them gripped him by the shoulder.

Gaskell spun around on his stool, his hand already inside his jacket and gripping the butt of his revolver.

'Hey, easy there, Charlie Boy!' said one of the men.

Gaskell squinted in the hazy, blue-grey light of the smoking room and realised, very quickly, that he knew them. McQuaid and Tice, both of them crew members on HMS *Atropos*. McQuaid, a short and wiry Irishman, had been the gunner, while Tice, a towering near-giant of a man, had served alongside Gaskell in the Marines. He hadn't seen them in three years or more.

'McQuaid?' Gaskell said, smiling quizzically. 'Tice? What are you doing here?'

'Could ask the same of you!' said McQuaid, still gripping Gaskell by the shoulder. 'I mean, look at you, in your fancy suit and your fancy hat. Somebody landed on their feet when they came ashore, didn't they?'

Gaskell laughed a little nervously. His eyes met Tice's for a moment, but the taller man said nothing.

'So what line of work's got you all dolled up like the Prince of Wales?' asked McQuaid. 'Are you selling Bibles or something?'

'It's Government work,' Gaskell replied, evasively.

McQuaid turned to Tice, raising both eyebrows. 'D'you hear that, Tice?' he said. '*Government* work! Well I never. Government work, he says. And, no offence, like, but they're letting *coloured* fellas do Government work now, are they?'

Gaskell narrowed his eyes. Where was this leading? What were they doing there? He couldn't accept that it was merely a coincidence. He nodded silently in reply.

'Well fancy that!' said McQuaid, his tone bordering on sarcasm. 'They'll be letting the Irish in on the game soon, eh, Tice? Maybe get myself a job as a civil servant, what d'you reckon?'

Tice laughed through his nose with a huff, but said nothing.

Gaskell rose from his stool. 'Well, gents,' he said. 'I was just leaving.'

'Leaving already?' said McQuaid. 'But we've only just got here, so we have.'

'Sorry, McQuaid. Maybe some other time.'

Gaskell turned to Clara and nodded a silent goodbye, then offered a brief nod to McQuaid and Tice in turn, before leaving the Six Bells.

It was as he walked along Charlotte Street that he realised he was being followed. McQuaid and Tice were behind him, keeping their distance, but following him nonetheless.

Gaskell turned off Charlotte Street and into an alleyway lined on both sides with barrels and crates. The far end of the alley met a dead end at the back of the Bute Street slaughterhouse, but he already knew this. It was part of his plan. When he had almost reached the end of the alley he turned on his heels to see McQuaid and Tice standing between the barrels and blocking his escape, both of them brandishing knives.

'You know,' said McQuaid, 'you're a good sort, Charlie Boy. It's a crying shame we've got to do this, but times are hard, you know?'

'Who sent you?' demanded Gaskell.

'Now that would be telling.' McQuaid smirked. 'Maybe it's a jealous husband, or *maybe* it's someone who thinks you ask too many questions. Who are we to say?'

They were walking towards him now, Tice still silent, McQuaid turning the knife over and over in his hand.

Gaskell reached inside his jacket and drew his revolver from its holster. McQuaid and Tice both stopped in their tracks.

'Oh, come now, Charlie Boy,' said McQuaid. 'That's not exactly sporting, is it? We bring knives and you bring a gun? You been reading too many of them stories about the Wild West now, haven't you? Fancying yourself as a regular Wild Bill Hickok?'

'Fine,' said Gaskell, placing the revolver down onto a barrel. 'Suit yourselves.'

McQuaid smiled malevolently, nodded, and then, after only a moment's pause, he and Tice came forward.

Gaskell bunched his hands into fists and adopted the stance of a boxer, resting back on his heels as they drew closer and closer.

Tice was in front, now. Practically mute though he may have been, he was the brawn to back up McQuaid's sarcastic wit, the secret, silent weapon in his arsenal.

Gaskell waited, and waited, and, when Tice was only a few feet away from him, he spun around, his left leg arcing up in one fluid motion until his booted foot slammed violently into Tice's jaw with a loud crack.

Tice staggered sideways, falling into a tower of barrels which came crashing down around him, but Gaskell was far from finished.

As McQuaid made his move, the blade of his knife held out like a poor man's rapier, Gaskell dodged to one side and then delivered a crippling punch to the Irishman's ribs. McQuaid gasped for air and lunged again but Gaskell grabbed his wrist and in one swift move snapped it with a sickening crunch.

McQuaid swore, dropping the knife to the ground, his hand hanging limp and twisted at his side.

Tice was back on his feet, slack-jawed but conscious, and, as he came running forward, Gaskell delivered another kick to his face and then, before he had a chance to recover, a punishing blow to Tice's stomach.

Scrambling around on his hands and knees, McQuaid searched the puddles and potholes for his knife. As he spotted it and made a grab for the handle, Gaskell kicked him in the head and then the stomach, pinning him to the ground with his boot against the Irishman's throat.

'Who sent you?' Gaskell snarled.

McQuaid looked up at him, his lips curled into a bloodied sneer, and laughed.

'Who sent you?' Gaskell asked once more.

From somewhere behind him Gaskell heard the sound of sluggish footsteps sloshing through the puddles. Without taking his foot from McQuaid's throat and without turning, he reached out, grabbed his revolver from where he had left it, aimed it back over his shoulder and fired.

A second later he heard the sound of Tice's corpse hitting the ground with a heavy thud.

He aimed the gun down at McQuaid.

'Tell me who sent you,' he said, through gritted teeth.

McQuaid laughed again. 'Loud gunshot like that,' he whispered, blood and saliva foaming in the corner of his mouth. 'Somebody'll have called the police…'

'Who *sent* you?'

'I'm not telling *you*,' McQuaid cackled. 'You'll have to shoot me first.'

Gaskell looked McQuaid in the eyes, searching for just a flicker of hesitation, but he saw none. McQuaid meant every word of what he said. Gaskell thumbed back the hammer of his pistol and aimed it squarely at McQuaid's forehead.

Somewhere beyond the alleyway, out on the thoroughfare of Charlotte Street, he could hear the sound of police whistles. The last thing Gaskell needed was to waste time with the police, as much as he might enjoy watching constables grudgingly acknowledge his authority.

Without a moment's hesitation, he opened his revolver and

emptied the five remaining shells into the palm of his hand, pocketing them as he did so. Then, using a handkerchief, he wiped down the butt of the pistol, and crouching on his haunches placed it on the ground next to McQuaid.

'Bastard…' McQuaid hissed.

Gaskell looked down at him and winked.

'You should have answered my question.'

He was far away from the alleyway and Charlotte Street by the time the police arrived.

As night fell, a wall of fog came rolling in over the docks and the tangled streets of Butetown. The skeletal masts of tall ships were all that could be seen rising up out of the mist, and the sound of foghorns echoed across the town like a mournful lullaby.

Deep under the ink-black waters of the Oval Basin, three people prepared themselves for the night ahead.

Emily Holroyd loaded her Smith and Wesson revolver, checking the action several times over before sliding it into her holster.

Alice Guppy sharpened her Corsican vendetta knife on a whetstone.

Charles Gaskell opened the cupboard next to his desk and lifted out his Winchester pump-action shotgun.

As if acting upon some unspoken signal they rose from their stations and together they marched along the narrow corridor from the Hub to the stables.

Moments later, on a street shrouded in fog, an anonymous wooden door in an abandoned warehouse opened with mechanical grace, and from the darkness inside three horses and their riders came charging out into the night.

They rode through streets filled with shadows and fog, past the spectral lights of taverns and ghostly figures half-hidden in doorways. They passed beneath the dank and dripping underside of a bridge as a cargo train laden with coal howled over them. They followed the banks of the canal, past barges and narrowboats and scurrying black mischiefs of water rats. They rode on and on into the night, through narrow cobbled streets like ancient canyons, until they came at last to the river and the great black hulk of HMS *Hades*.

The ship appeared to them through the fog like some monster from an ancient legend, the flickering lights in its smoke-blackened windows like menacing eyes blinking in the gloom.

Gaskell, Emily and Alice slowed their horses to a canter and came to a halt when they were a safe distance from the crumbling wreck. After dismounting they tethered the horses, and made their way very slowly towards the ship.

'Remember,' said Emily as they neared its hull, 'caution at all times. There may be children on board.'

'And we don't even know what we're looking for,' Gaskell muttered. 'We might be chasing after the fantasies of a paranoid old fool.'

'Do you think so?' said Emily. 'Well, he was a paranoid old fool someone saw fit to murder and dismember. Captain Harkness is still missing. And *then* we have the matter of your little altercation this afternoon…'

Gaskell stopped in his tracks and turned to face her.

'Oh, you thought I wouldn't find out about that?' said Emily, raising an eyebrow. 'You forget, Mr Gaskell, that there is a reason I run our operations. Don't worry… You shan't be reprimanded for your actions. My only question is this… If McQuaid and Tice were old friends of yours from your naval days, do you still believe Montague has no involvement in this?'

'What happened this afternoon proves nothing,' Gaskell snapped. 'And we don't even know what *this* is…'

'Well,' said Emily, walking ahead of him, 'I rather think we're about to find out.'

Treading carefully, she made her way down the riverbank until she was standing directly below the edge of the *Hades'* portside deck. From her satchel she produced a small pistol, in the barrel of which there sat an iron grappling hook. She aimed the gun and fired, the hook silently launching itself up and over the ship's side at the end of a length of rope. With a forceful tug, Emily pulled the rope tight and began to climb up the side of the ship, Alice following close behind her.

'You know, we could have tried knocking at the door,' said Gaskell, shaking his head as he grasped the rope and joined them.

Emily was first onto the deck, with Alice and Gaskell hoisting themselves over the edge only a few seconds later.

'Yes,' Emily whispered. 'But that wouldn't be as much fun, now, would it?'

Gaskell was about to reply when he saw a shadowy figure emerging from a trapdoor and running very suddenly and silently towards them. He drew his shotgun from its scabbard, worked its pump-action, and fired.

The muzzle flare lit up the deck like a flash of lightning, while the gunshot rumbled and echoed out into the night like thunder. The shadowy figure was hurled backward, hitting the deck with a heavy thud.

Emily and Alice turned to Gaskell, Alice cupping her hand over one ear and wincing.

'Mr Gaskell!' cried Emily. 'I believe I told you to practise caution…'

He pushed past them to where the body had fallen. Though the assailant's face had been virtually destroyed by the blast of the shotgun, it was instantly apparent that he, or *it*, was not human. The crest of thin flesh on the crown of its head and the spiny fins around its jowls were all too familiar to them.

'It's a *homoformatus piscis*…' said Emily.

Alice and Gaskell looked at her with raised eyebrows.

'Well,' said Emily, 'when either of you can think of a better name for them, I'll be more than happy to hear it.'

'But what's it doing *here*?' asked Alice. '*Guarding* this place?'

Gaskell crouched down beside the body. Around its neck it wore a heavy brass collar in the centre of which was an ovoid vial filled with blue liquid.

'What is that?' asked Emily.

Without answering her, Gaskell used the stock of his shotgun to shatter the vial. All at once the air was filled with the scent of almonds.

'Cyanide…' said Gaskell.

Careful not to touch any of the liquid he lifted the collar away from the creature's throat. Its inside edge was lined with tiny needles, barely visible to the naked eye.

'It must be some kind of device for controlling them,' he said.

'Then there may be others,' said Emily.

Gaskell looked up at her and nodded.

Leaving the body where it lay, they explored the deck of the *Hades*, winding their way through the tight maze of walkways between its ramshackle buildings. Eventually they came to a door through which they saw the dim traces of lamplight.

'Miss Guppy,' said Emily, pointing to the lock. 'If you would?'

Alice nodded and set at once about picking the lock with her hairpin. After only a few seconds she heard the satisfying clunk as its bolt slid back, and the door creaked open. Emily nodded to Alice and Gaskell in turn and then led them through the doorway into a barely lit stairwell.

Down and down they walked, treading as silently as they could on steps that creaked and groaned with every footfall, until they came at last to a long wooden corridor lined on one side with flickering oil lamps. As they edged their way along the passage Gaskell drew his shotgun and lifted it up, aiming it squarely at the far end of the corridor.

From somewhere on the other side of a door they could hear the sound of footsteps. They stopped walking, Emily placing her forefinger to her lips.

A moment's silence, the three of them holding their

breath as one and waiting, and then the sound of the door handle being turned…

The door opened suddenly and violently with a crash, and another one of the amphibious creatures came running out of the shadows.

Gaskell lifted up his shotgun and took aim but, before he could fire, Alice had drawn and thrown her knife. The blade spun through the air, end over end, until it buried itself in their assailant's eye. The creature stopped in its tracks and staggered back, clumsily clutching at the knife's handle in the last, desperate seconds before it fell to the ground and died.

Gaskell breathed out loudly, lowering his shotgun.

'Do you see, Mr Gaskell?' said Emily. 'These things *can* be done quietly, you know.'

Alice ran to the dead alien and pulled the blade from its eye, wiping it clean on her coat before returning it to her pocket. She was about to stand when a second creature emerged from the doorway, brandishing a cleaver.

Gaskell lifted his shotgun for the second time in as many minutes, his finger curled around the trigger, and took aim.

Suddenly the corridor was filled with the deafening racket of a single gunshot. The creature was hit in the chest and thrown to the ground, where it lay writhing and twitching in the throes of death.

Emily Holroyd blew the gun smoke from the barrel of her pistol and slid it back into its holster.

'You were saying?' said Gaskell.

***

'They are here,' said the Widow Blight, standing in the doorway of his study.

Sat behind his desk with a smile that Mrs Blight had not expected, Tiberius Finch clasped his hands together and nodded sagely.

'Yes they are,' he said. 'But they will run out of ammunition soon enough. They are no match for our specimens.' Rising to his feet, he opened a drawer and lifted out his revolver.

'Surely you are not considering confronting them yourself?' asked Mrs Blight.

'Not at all,' Finch replied. 'This is merely a precaution. We must go to our patient at once. Those fools do not know the ship as well as we do. They will quickly find themselves quite lost and outnumbered.'

'But the babies… What if they find the babies?'

'Let them,' Finch replied. 'We have a more valuable asset now. To the laboratory…'

Alice Guppy kicked the creature in its face, sending it reeling backwards, stunned. As it prepared itself for another attack, Charles Gaskell lifted his shotgun and blasted it in the chest. There was not a second's pause before another one of the creatures came lumbering towards them, its hands reaching out with murderous intent. Emily Holroyd took aim with her revolver, and killed it with a single shot.

They had arrived at a wooden door many levels below the deck of the HMS *Hades* and had killed almost a dozen of the creatures, but now there was silence.

Alice set about picking the door's lock, and seconds

later they entered a stygian chamber filled with empty cots. Using her flashlight, Emily cast a single prism of yellow light around the bare and desolate room. There were traces of old blood on the floorboards, and in one corner of the room a pile of fabrics.

'What is it?' asked Alice.

Emily approached the pile, and crouched to pick up one of the bundles of cloth. It was a child's blanket. She gasped, dropping it to the ground. Beside the pile of blankets was another mound, this time consisting of nothing but children's shoes. Dozens and dozens of children's shoes.

'Where are the children?' asked Gaskell. 'This place is like a nursery, but where are the children?'

Emily didn't answer him. She rose to her feet and crossed the darkened room to a second door. Placing her ear against the wood, she heard sounds coming from the other side, a strange mewling, like the mournful wailing of cats.

She tried the handle. The door was unlocked, and so she opened it very slowly. Through it there was a second chamber, this one illuminated by thin beams of pale blue moonlight that spilled in through grimy portholes. Like the first room this one was also filled with cots, perhaps fifty of them in all, but these were occupied. As she gazed down into the first cot she came across, Emily saw, wriggling on its back and shackled to the cot's frame, an alien infant. The creature looked up at her and hissed, gnashing its teeth and clawing helplessly at the air.

'Dear Lord,' said Alice, walking past row after row of cots. 'What are they *doing* here?'

'They're *breeding* them,' replied Emily. 'That first room… the nursery…'

Alice looked at her. She saw in Emily's expression something she had never seen before: a palpable horror, laced with an immeasurable sadness. Tears welled in her eyes.

'What is it?' asked Alice

'It wasn't a nursery,' replied Emily. 'It was where they *fed*.'

'Who?'

Emily looked down into the cots, at the wailing, shackled creatures that surrounded them, and Alice understood all too well what she meant.

'Dear God…' she said.

Gaskell stood at the next door, shaking his head, his eyes screwed shut as if he dared not look at the monstrous infants a second longer. When they had composed themselves they moved on, into a narrow stairwell that led further down into the depths of the *Hades*. They came at last to a dark and dank room with no illumination. Using the flashlight once more, Emily shone its beam across the room and they saw that it was furnished with cylindrical glass tanks.

Each tank was filled with murky water, and suspended in the cloudy liquid the twisted forms of alien foetuses. Some were recognisable as the amphibious creatures that had been shackled in the cots, others were unlike anything they had seen before. In one they saw a pitiful specimen with finned jowls and clawed hands, but what looked all too much like human hair.

Emily could hardly breathe. She felt appalled and nauseous at the same time, the mounting horror of the situation almost too much to bear. Taking a deep breath and letting it out slowly, she moved on, Gaskell and Alice close behind her, into another narrow wooden corridor. At the end of this passage was yet another wooden door in the centre of which was a small window. Through its grubby, warped glass could be seen the flickering yellow glow of lamplight. Emily approached the door as silently as she could, and gazed through it.

On the other side was a room that might once have served as the armoury of HMS *Hades*, its walls lined with empty gun racks, and in one corner a row of rusting harpoons. Now, it would appear, it served a different purpose. In the centre of the room was a surgeon's operating table surrounded by numerous scientific apparatus: burners and glass jars filled with mysterious chemicals; a tray filled with surgical instruments.

Standing beside the table, Emily saw the figures of Mrs Blight and Tiberius Finch. They were hunched over a figure who was strapped to the table by his hands and wrists. Only when the Widow Blight moved a little to one side did Emily see that the man strapped to the table was Jack Harkness.

'They have him,' she whispered to the others. 'Captain Harkness…'

She leaned closer to the door, tilting her ear toward the window, and listened.

'It would appear your friends are here to *rescue* you,' said Finch with a derisive laugh. 'They shan't last very long. Tonight will prove a useful demonstration of our experiment's worth. Meanwhile, you are our most prized

50

asset, Captain Harkness, and as such we feel it would be wise to move you to another location. Sir Henry will pay very handsomely for a specimen such as yourself.'

Emily turned to Gaskell. It was clear he had heard every word Finch had said. She looked through the window once more.

'Mrs Blight,' said Finch, turning to his accomplice. 'The chloroform, if you please…'

'What are we waiting for?' hissed Gaskell, pulling Emily out of the way.

'Mr Gaskell!' snapped Emily, but it was too late.

With a forceful kick, Gaskell opened the door to Finch's makeshift laboratory, and charged into the room, working the pump-action of his shotgun as he did so.

Finch spun around, diving out of Gaskell's aim as the thunderous blast of the shotgun punched a hole through the wooden wall behind him. He drew his pistol, and, hitting the deck with a thud, he fired a single shot which slammed into Gaskell's chest, throwing him back into the darkness of the corridor.

Gathering himself as quickly as he could, Finch got to his feet and fired another shot through the doorway, before fleeing for a second door. He turned and fired a third time before he disappeared into the shadows.

Cursing under her breath, Mrs Blight set about dousing a cloth with chloroform but, before she could place it over Jack's mouth, she was joined by Emily, Alice and Gaskell.

'You were shot! I saw it!' she hissed at Gaskell. She pointed down at Jack. 'You're… you're like *him*!'

Gaskell shook his head, tapping his chest with his fist. It sounded as if his ribs were made of wood.

'The benefits of a bullet-proof vest,' he said with a confident grin. He turned to Jack. 'You all right?'

'Oh yeah,' said Jack. 'I'm great. A little tied up at the moment, but that's not always a bad thing…'

Emily turned to Gaskell. 'Find Finch,' she said. 'Don't let him leave the ship.'

Gaskell nodded, running from the room with his shotgun at his side, and then Alice and Emily turned to the Widow Blight.

'Mrs Blight,' said Emily. 'In the name of Her Majesty, Queen Victoria, I—'

Mrs Blight hit her in the face with a brutal left hook.

Shocked and dazed, Emily fell back against the operating table, stemming the flow of blood from her nose with the back of her hand.

Alice looked from Emily to the Widow Blight and shook her head. 'Oh, you have just made one *very* big mistake,' she said, edging her way toward Mrs Blight, her fists raised.

Having gathered her wits, Emily began undoing the straps that held Jack Harkness to the table. 'Sorry if I'm ruining your fun, Captain Harkness,' she said.

'Not at all, Miss Holroyd,' replied Jack with a wink.

Alice and the Widow Blight were now in one corner of the laboratory, the latter trapped between the operating table and the far wall. Mrs Blight looked around the room as if searching for some means of escape, and then, with a monstrous howl, she launched herself at Alice, her bony hands reaching for the younger woman's throat. Clawing at her with jagged fingernails, Mrs Blight knocked Alice to the ground and together they fought on the floor of the laboratory, hitting shelves and racks filled with instruments. Glass jars and vials tumbled to the ground, where they shattered, their liquid contents splashing onto rough wood, and still the two women fought.

Alice pushed the older woman away from her and stood. For a moment they faced one another from either side of the room, before coming together once more, punching and slapping one another with brutal force.

As Emily freed Jack from the table, and helped him to his feet, the Widow Blight grabbed Alice by the throat and pushed her down onto the operating table. Emily turned to them and drew her gun, but before she could fire a single shot Alice had lifted up her legs and kicked Mrs Blight in the stomach with all her strength.

The older woman reeled, wheezing and spluttering and doubled over in pain. The soles of her shoes crunched against broken glass and then all at once she lost her footing on the slippery surface and was sent staggering back toward the row of harpoons, her arms flailing wildly and her eyes wide with panic. A rusty spike erupted from her chest with a sickening squelch, and she stared down at the blade in horror, a thin stream of blood trickling from the corner of her mouth. Desperately she gasped for air, once, twice.

The third gasp was her last.

After a moment's silence, they heard footsteps. The door swung open with a crash, and Gaskell ran into the room.

Seeing Mrs Blight's corpse, he grimaced before turning to Jack, Emily and Alice.

'I've lost Finch,' he said. 'This place is a labyrinth.'

'Then we need to get off the ship,' said Emily. 'He may have escaped.'

Together they ran from the laboratory, back through the network of corridors and stairwells until they came to the gloomy nursery where alien children gurgled in their cots. As Emily and Alice carried on running, Jack set about breaking the bars of the cots and releasing them from their shackles.

'What on Earth are you doing?' asked Gaskell. 'Harkness? Are you listening to me?'

'We've got to free them,' said Jack. 'They're just children.'

Gaskell laughed anxiously. 'Are you out of your mind?' he said. 'Those aren't children, Harkness. They are *aliens*.'

But Jack didn't listen. As the others ran on, he continued in his task until all of the cots were broken and all of the creatures freed.

One by one the infants lowered themselves from their cots and began to gather around him, gnashing their teeth.

'OK,' said Jack. 'Maybe not the best idea I ever had...'

Turning on his heels, he ran after the others as quickly as he could, slamming the nursery door shut behind him.

On the deck of HMS *Hades*, hiding behind a barrel and a mound of old rope, Tiberius Finch watched as the four members of Torchwood fled from the ship and gathered themselves on the riverbank. Though they were too far away for him to hear their voices, they seemed to be in some state of panic. Perhaps they had finally found themselves outnumbered by his personal guard. He certainly liked to think so.

The events of that evening were, he had decided, but a minor hindrance. His research had proven fruitful. However powerful Torchwood might consider themselves, they had overstepped the mark, and by quite some way. When those who had funded his experiments were told what had happened, the Torchwood Institute would be made to pay, and dearly.

Laughing softly to himself, Finch rested with his back against the barrel. He wondered what had happened to the Widow Blight, and felt a brief pang of melancholy at the thought that she had probably perished. It passed very quickly. There are few great acts achieved without sacrifice. Harkness's escape and Mrs Blight's death, he decided, were two such sacrifices.

As he drifted into a reverie, plotting his next moves and whatever revenge might be had against Torchwood, Tiberius Finch heard something scuttling across the deck.

He sat up straight and peered into the shadows, but saw nothing.

And then, once more, he heard it. Like the sound of a dozen feet tapping their way across the wooden floor.

'Hello?' he murmured. 'Who goes there?'

Now, at last, he saw something. Tiny shapes moving in the darkness, illuminated only briefly by the occasional shifting beams of moonlight that broke through the clouds.

'Hello…?' Finch said once more, but still there was no reply.

Rising from his hiding place, Finch crossed the deck towards the shadowy forms. They were gathered around an open trapdoor, and as he neared them he saw that they were increasing in number. Only when he was a few short steps away from them did he realise who – or what – they were.

They were his specimens.

However monstrous and bizarre they might be, he knew that they were intelligent, at least as intelligent as human children if not more so. He knew, gazing into their obsidian black eyes, that they recognised him. More than this, he knew, as they began to surround him, that they were hungry for revenge.

From the riverbank they heard the sounds of screaming on the deck of the *Hades* and looked up.

'Finch…' said Gaskell.

'Sounds like his pupils caught up with him,' said Jack. He turned to the others. 'We should leave. There are too many of those things on board the ship. We can't hope to catch them all. We need back-up, or the proper equipment, or…'

'Well we wouldn't need *any* of those things if you hadn't released them all,' said Gaskell, approaching his horse, 'Besides… I have a better idea.'

He reached into the saddlebag and pulled out a short glass tube at the end of which was a fuse.

Jack looked at his colleague, and at the glass tube, shaking his head. 'You wouldn't…' he said.

'Just watch me, Harkness,' said Gaskell, lighting the fuse and then hurling the tube at HMS *Hades*.

As the projectile hit the deck of the old ship there was a sudden flash of light and then, in an instant, a blanket of fire had engulfed one of its ramshackle structures.

'But they're just *children*…' said Jack.

Gaskell turned to him, simmering with anger. 'They're vermin,' he snapped. 'A pest to be exterminated. Nothing more.'

Jack launched himself at Gaskell but was held back by Emily.

'Gentlemen,' she said. 'Do you really think this is the time or the place?'

She looked up at the ship, which was now half ablaze. The rooftops of its shacks were caving in, the innards of the boat groaning and roaring as the fire consumed it deck by deck. Somewhere, beyond the roar of the flames, they could hear the sound of the creatures screaming.

Jack eyeballed Gaskell, his expression still one of fury. Breaking away from Emily's grasp he turned his back and walked away from them.

'Where do you think you're going?' Alice cried after him.

Jack stopped and glanced back over his shoulder.

'Like I told you,' he said. 'I'm freelance.'

He looked at Alice, then Emily, and Gaskell in turn, still seething with anger, and then he carried on walking until he had vanished like a spectre into the mist.

As chunks of burning debris rained down into the ink-black water, Gaskell, Alice and Emily mounted their horses, and rode out into the night, leaving the flames and the wreckage and the screaming far behind them.

'I've been thinking,' said Alice, sipping from her cup of tea as she sat down at Emily's desk. 'What would have happened if *you* had met with Mayhew, and not Jack?'

Emily joined her, stirring her own cup three times before she sat.

'Whatever do you mean?'

'Well,' Alice continued, 'if you had met with Mayhew, then you… well… *you* would have died.'

Emily gazed up into a far corner of the room, deep in thought. 'Yes,' she said at last with a quizzical smile. 'I suppose I might have.'

There was a moment's pause between them, the office silent but for the ticking of a clock.

'So,' said Alice, 'what would have happened then?'

'I don't think I follow you…'

'Well… Who would have taken your place?'

Emily let out a short, incredulous laugh. 'Really, Alice,' she said. 'I thought you might have been a little more concerned for my wellbeing, or that you would have missed me for other reasons…'

Alice smiled. 'Well of course there's *that*,' she said, and then, her expression grew pensive again. 'Yes… I don't know what I'd do without you. You know that.'

'I know.'

'But it still leaves the question… What would we do?'

Emily nodded thoughtfully.

'Indeed,' she said, after an age. 'It's a good point, Alice. A very good point indeed, and one which needs addressing. But perhaps we should leave it until the morning. It *has* been a very long day, has it not?'

Alice smiled.

'And,' Emily continued, 'I am sure there are far more enjoyable things with which we can occupy ourselves this evening.'

'Why, Miss Holroyd,' said Alice, raising one eyebrow. 'Whatever do you mean?'

Emily leaned across the desk and kissed her gently on the lips.

'I shall leave *that* to your imagination, Miss Guppy,' she replied.

Clara mopped down the last table with a damp and dirty cloth and wiped her brow with the back of her hand. Another day was over, the last customers now staggering their way home along Charlotte Street. She tilted her head from side to side with a click and yawned.

Behind her, the door opened and the bell above it jangled.

'I'm sorry,' she said. 'We're closed for the night. You'll have to get your ale elsewhere…'

'I wasn't looking for ale.'

She turned and saw Charles Gaskell standing in the doorway.

'Oh, Charlie!' she said, laughing. 'You almost gave me a fright there!'

She expected him to smile back at her, but he didn't. Instead, he crossed the room and put his arms around her, sighing heavily. Dropping the damp cloth to the ground, she held him, and kissed his cheek. He held her even more tightly than before and let out another sigh.

'Bad day?' she asked.

Gaskell said nothing, but simply nodded.

'And you still won't tell me anything about it, will you?'

He shook his head.

Clara looked into his eyes. They were filled with an inscrutable sadness. He looked down at the floor, his forehead against hers, and she kissed him once more.

'That's all right,' she said, touching his cheek and smiling. 'It's all right.'

Admiral Sir Henry Montague wound the handle of his gramophone until its turntable began to spin, and dropped the needle gently onto the revolving vinyl disc. After a moment's faint crackling, his study was filled with the opening bars of the adagio from Schubert's String Quintet.

He crossed the study and stood in its bay window, gazing out at the fields of Penarth's headland. In the distance, looking no larger than a child's bath-time toys, ships made their way in and out of Cardiff's docks, the water around them lit up crimson by the rising sun

This moment of tranquillity was interrupted by the sound of someone entering the room.

He turned very quickly and saw, standing at the other side of his desk, Captain Jack Harkness.

'I'm sorry,' said Montague. 'But who are you?'

'You know who I am,' said Jack, coldly. 'Now sit down.'

'Phillips!' Montague bellowed. 'Phillips! Where the devil are you?'

'Phillips isn't here,' said Jack. 'I've given him the day off. Now *sit*.'

Eyeing Jack cautiously, and biting his lip, Montague sat behind his desk. 'What do you want?' he asked.

Jack helped himself to the facing chair and folded his arms.

'I know all about the *Hades*,' he said. 'I know *all* about your little scheme.'

'I'm afraid I haven't the slightest idea what you're talking about,' said Montague.

Jack rose, leaning across the table.

'Finch and Blight were capturing and breeding aliens, and they were breeding them for *you*,' he said. 'Sound familiar?'

Montague narrowed his eyes, staring straight back at Jack, and then he smiled.

'I see,' he said. 'And from whom exactly did you glean this information?'

'I didn't *glean* it from anyone,' said Jack. 'I was there. I saw it for myself. They were breeding aliens, and taking children from desperate mothers. They were carrying out *experiments*. And you were the one paying for it all. The only thing I can't work out is *why*.'

Montague sat back in his chair and laughed. 'So Torchwood really *are* employing the brightest and best,' he said, derisively. 'Captain Harkness, my dear fellow… There are forces at work in this world which you can barely comprehend.'

'Oh, I doubt that…'

'You think I'm talking about those creatures? Those fantastical beasts that spill out into our world from God alone knows where?' He laughed again. 'Oh, I'm not talking about ghouls and goblins, or whatever one might wish to call them. I'm talking about mankind. Of all creatures, on this world or any other, mankind is the most dangerous. He is the greatest threat to no one but himself. There are many who wish to wreak havoc upon this sceptred isle, Captain Harkness. Our enemies are great in number. There is a storm coming, you mark my words. A war, the like of which we have never seen before. I'm a warrior at heart, and a warrior can feel it in his bones.

'The instruments of this war are already being made. The machine gun… The submarine… Gases that will blind and poison and kill. We will need every weapon available to us if we are to win such a war. Imagine, Captain Harkness, if you will, an army of amphibious assassins with strength ten times greater than their human adversaries. What other creatures might we find who we can render servile and prepare for war?'

Jack looked at Montague in horror. 'An army,' he said, in disbelief. 'You were breeding an army…'

Montague nodded, still smiling. 'When this war is with us,' he said, 'who would you rather see die on its battlefields? These sub-human wretches from the far-flung reaches of the universe, or England's schoolboys? I know which I would choose.'

Jack got to his feet. 'You know,' he said, 'you're right about the war, I'll give you that. The only thing you got wrong is this… The next war, and many of the ones that follow… They won't be fought in the name of men like you. They'll be fought *against* them. You won't get away with this…'

Montague laughed. 'Oh, really? And who exactly are you going to tell, Captain Harkness? HMS *Hades* lies smouldering on the banks of the River Taff. The specimens are little more than ashes. Tiberius Finch and the Widow Blight are dead. I am a knight of the realm, you fool. You know as well as I do that the authorities and your superiors would rather this were covered up discreetly. My research *will* continue.'

'I don't think so,' said Jack.

'Is that so?' said Montague. 'And what makes you so sure?'

Jack turned and opened the study door. Before leaving the room, he turned back to face the Admiral.

'You didn't just make *us* your enemies last night, Montague,' he said, smiling coldly.

Montague looked out through the door and saw two figures standing in the hallway. They walked into the study, each nodding to Harkness in turn.

Montague gasped.

Standing before him, dressed in three-piece suits, were two monstrous creatures, their smooth, amphibious heads crowned with rigid crests of thin flesh, their shapeless mouths filled with tiny, pin-like teeth.

'Dear God…' Montague gasped.

Jack looked from the creatures to Montague then, turning

63

his back on them, closed the study door behind him. As he walked along the hallway, through the multicoloured prisms of light from the stained-glass window, the haunting melody of Schubert's Adagio was drowned out by the sound of one man screaming.

Kaleidoscope

SARAH PINBOROUGH

The boy's heart thumped.

'I said get out here, Danny!' The beast raged through the walls of the unkempt council flat. 'You bloody deaf, boy?'

Danny Dillard shivered as he sat on the end of his bed. His dad's words ran together into one long slurred sentence that was filled with anger and hatred and emotions that Danny wasn't sure he'd ever understand, or want to. He licked his lips, his eyes wide. He should have stayed out. He should have gone and hidden in the corner of the community centre and done his homework or read a book or just sat there. If he hadn't come straight home from school, then he wouldn't have knocked his dad's unwashed mug from the kitchen side and broken it. They only had two. His dad refused to buy any more. And now they were down to one.

'Don't make me come in there and get you, Danny!' The snarl made the boy flinch. 'Don't make me do that!'

Tears stung at the back of Danny's eyes, knowing what was to come. He got slowly to his feet and forced himself to the door.

'Sorry, Dad.' He stared up at the hulk of the man glowering down at him, his eyes glazed and red from too much time spent in the pub, *and filled with loathing. 'It was an accident.'*

'Waste of space, you are.' The man spat the words at the child as he raised one hand. 'Just like your no-good bloody mother, wherever the hell she is.'

The mention of the woman who'd just upped and left Danny here with the monster made his dad's eyes burn, and Danny squeezed his own shut. He knew what was coming. His arms rose protectively to his head, but they didn't stop his teeth rattling and stars flying across the backs of his eyelids as the first blow hit him squarely on the side of his head and sent him tumbling backwards onto the floor. He curled into a ball and wished himself away as he waited for the second to land. There was never just one.

As it was, Danny's dad took a while to calm down.

'I don't want it.'

Toshiko folded her arms and peered up through her fringe. 'I think Gwen should have it.'

On the other side of the table, Gwen's eyes widened. 'No way. I'm still the new girl.'

Toshiko raised an eyebrow.

'OK, maybe not so new any more,' Gwen conceded. 'But still the newest.'

The women's eyes fell back to the object in the middle of the table, staring at it just like Ianto and Owen opposite. The latter licked his lips.

'Well, if no one else wants it, then…'

'Not so fast.' Ianto stopped him before his hand could make a grab for it. 'I don't think you're cut out for that cup of coffee.' The two men glared at each other for a moment before their eyes fell again. Toshiko sighed.

'Look, if no one else wants it, then I don't see why I shouldn't have it.' Owen looked at the small group gathered round the table. 'I've got what it takes. I'm a born leader, everyone says so.'

The drink had started out hot, black and strong but had stayed untouched for so long a film was settling on its surface. It was Jack's coffee, and he hated it cold. But if Jack had been here then the coffee, and what it represented, wouldn't have been an issue.

'Right.' Gwen didn't hide her sarcasm. 'You're a born leader, all right. You nearly led us into the bloody Apocalypse. You're the one that insisted on opening the Rift. You almost killed Jack.'

Owen's mouth twitched, disgruntled. 'Well, you all followed me, didn't you?' He shrugged. 'That's got to be a sign of leadership.' No one answered. 'Hasn't it?'

'Clutching at straws there, Owen,' Gwen muttered. She tried to relax her jaw. Owen rankled with her, and she couldn't help it. Nearly losing Rhys in the recent madness created by opening the Rift had made her realise just how much she loved and needed her husband. She wasn't sure if this need to dig at Owen was because she blamed him for what had happened or because there was still a residue of sexual tension between them, but either way he was really pissing her off.

'It's not going to be you, Owen,' she said. 'So just sit down and get over it.'

'Look,' Toshiko cut in. 'Let's not argue. Let's decide this

logically.' Her eyes flitted nervously around the room. 'As long as it's not me.'

Gwen groaned. Owen sighed and turned away.

'Wait.'

None of them had even noticed that Ianto had buried himself behind a laptop until he looked up. 'I think I've found something.'

'Jack?' Gwen raised an eyebrow. 'Finding Jack might solve our problem.'

'I don't think you should joke about it.' Toshiko's eyes were wide. 'What if he never comes back?'

'Of course he'll come back. This is Captain Jack bloody Harkness we're talking about. He's just off being Jack somewhere.'

'Does anyone mind?' Ianto stared at the women. 'If I could just finish – *this*,' he pointed emphatically at the screen, 'might actually resolve things.'

'Light us up then, Ianto,' Owen grumbled. 'Trust you to find an answer in the computer.' He darted a look over his shoulder. 'I'm surprised Tosh didn't beat you to it.'

Gwen saw the flinch at the edge of the Japanese girl's eyes. Owen Harper could truly be a bastard sometimes. She and Toshiko didn't always see eye to eye, but Gwen had started to understand the other woman's qualities. And it didn't take a genius to see she was in love with their medical officer. Part of Gwen wondered why he didn't just sleep with her and put the shy, geeky woman out of her misery. It wasn't like he hadn't slept with just about every other woman he'd ever been left alone in a room with. The thought made her feel uncomfortable again.

'Gwen?'

She looked up to find the other three looking at her. 'Sorry, Ianto. Go ahead.'

'I don't know why you're asking her permission, she's not—'

'Owen!' Toshiko and Ianto both cut him off.

He raised his hands in supplication. 'I'm just saying…'

'We know what you're saying,' Ianto sighed. 'We know you want to be in charge. But apparently what you or any of us want, doesn't count. Apparently there are regulations to cover this situation.'

'What kind of regulations?' Owen frowned.

'Look.'

The three other remaining members of the Torchwood team gathered round and peered over Ianto's suited shoulders. Scrawled writing filled the screen as if it had been scratched there with an old-fashioned calligraphy pen.

'It's from an early Torchwood manifesto. Rules and Regulations, drawn up early in 1900 by Emily Holroyd. The original document has been scanned into the system.'

'I can't read that writing.' Owen grumbled. Ianto clicked a small icon, and the handwriting transformed into typescript.

'Voilà.'

'Smart arse.'

There was a moment of silence as four sets of eyes scanned down and then slowed as they read the appropriate paragraph.

'Oh gosh,' Toshiko Sato whispered.

'If you've got a swearword in you,' Gwen said, 'then maybe this is the time for it. Whether you like it or not, you're in charge.'

'But that's ridiculous!'

'I don't believe it,' Owen added.

'It's there in black and white. She's the longest-serving member of the team, therefore "in the continued absence of the commanding officer, and without written instruction to the contrary from the Torchwood Institute (London)", she takes over. She's got the most experience.' Ianto looked up and smiled at Tosh. 'And let's face it, there's only four of us. And we're all capable of taking the responsibility if we're pushed.'

Gwen wondered if he'd emphasised the last bit a little too much. Had he been waiting for someone to suggest he take over? Gentle Ianto? She couldn't see it. But then now they had Tosh as their leader; Tosh who hated conflict and tried to please all the people all the time. Especially Owen. They were in for some interesting times. Bloody Jack Harkness. They thought he'd died for good, and then just as suddenly as they'd realised he was still alive, he disappeared again. Still, it wasn't just her that missed him. They all did. It was like the light in their lives had temporarily gone out. But they were just going to have to make the best of it and get on with their work until he got back.

'Oh gosh,' Toshiko said again, staring glumly at the table. 'I don't even like black coffee.'

'Coffee's going to have to wait.' Ianto was staring at

something on the laptop.

They all headed back to the main computer mainframe in the centre of the Hub.

'Something's happening. There.' Toshiko pointed, confident in her familiar position surrounded by technology. 'We've got a burst of energy. Nothing the system recognises, so I'm guessing whatever's causing it is alien.'

'What part of town is that?' Gwen asked.

Toshiko's fingers flew across the keyboard. 'The Fenmere estate. Down past the docks.'

'Not a nice part of town,' Owen said. 'Maybe you should stay here. Me and Ianto will…'

'Oh that's right,' Gwen cut in. 'Leave the ladies behind? Jack would love that. You're not in charge, remember?'

'No, and neither are you, so stop trying to—'

'Enough!' Ianto rarely raised his voice and the single word was enough to shut both Gwen and Owen up. 'I'll stay here. Tosh, you'd better go with these two.'

Toshiko looked hesitant before taking a shaky breath and drawing herself up tall. It should have made her appear confident. Somehow, she just looked more nervous. 'OK. Right. Let's go. Gwen, you drive.'

At least Owen didn't argue that.

Ianto toyed with the change in his pocket as he watched the others leave, trying his best to ignore the silence descending on the Hub. He wished he was with them, not because he wanted to bang all their heads together and remind them how lucky they all were to have each other – although he did really want to do that – but because there were just too many personal ghosts in the quiet spaces around him. His eyes snagged on Jack's office door. That space especially.

His shoulders slumped slightly and he felt the ache inside, right in the pit of his stomach, that left him feeling slightly sick. It was there most days, and always when he was in the Hub. This was Jack's place, and it was empty without him, they all knew that. Ianto could still hear the echo of his laugh and the feel of those hands on his skin. They'd tentatively been starting something that had the potential to be something great when Jack had gone, Ianto was sure of it. And it may have been Gwen who'd sat by Jack Harkness's side until he woke up, but it had been Ianto who had torn the place apart hunting for him after he'd gone.

Even when he'd realised that the hand in the jar had vanished, it had taken some time to convince him that Jack Harkness had gone on some kind of adventure without them – without him – and without even saying goodbye.

He stared at the office door and wished he could see the dark shape of the familiar greatcoat hanging on the other side. His heart ached. Jack Harkness. Where the bloody hell was he, and when was he coming back?

The Fenmere Estate was the kind of place that would be drab on a perfect summer afternoon; under a grey sky it looked positively bleak. The SUV parked up by the small promenade of tatty shops, most of which were either boarded over or had grilles pulled down and graffiti daubed across them.

The three members of the team got out and peered around them.

'Nice,' Owen muttered. Over by some railings separating the three large tower blocks from the shopping area, a group of teenage boys stared at them and then laughed. The tallest flicked a cigarette butt in their direction and stared defiantly.

'Let's get this done quickly, shall we?' Gwen said.

'The signal's coming from one of the shops over there.' Toshiko peered at small handheld device and then looked up again. 'That one.'

'At least it looks open.' Owen stepped forward.

Three metal balls that might once have been gold hung from the side of the pebble-dashed concrete building. They looked out of place against the backdrop and the rest of the shopfront failed to make them feel welcome. A single word, 'Pawnbroker', was printed efficiently in cracked black on the awning above the door, the letters large and unfussy so even the least educated amongst the local residents could read it clearly. Wide metal bars were permanently fixed at regular spaces across the windows to stop any would-be thieves attempting a smash and grab.

Gwen glanced in as they headed for the door. The contents of the display would make for a pathetic haul – an old electric guitar, a microwave, a DVD player and a Victorian vase – but she knew from her time in the police that there would be plenty of people willing to give it a go.

A bell rang as they stepped inside, and a man in his fifties shuffled out from a room at the back, bringing a small cloud of cigarette smoke with him.

'What you selling?' His narrow eyes ran over them expertly, lingering for a second on Gwen's leather jacket.

'Just looking, thanks.' Toshiko flashed him a brief smile, before Owen stood between her and the man's view so she could scan the room uninterrupted.

'Those items on that side are for sale.' The old man sniffed. 'Just so you know.'

'There,' Toshiko whispered, and the small group gathered by a display case in the corner.

Owen frowned. 'What is it?'

Gwen slid the plastic door back and picked the object up. It looked like a telescope, long and cylindrical. It was heavy; a lump of weight in her hands that felt like dense metal rather than the wood it appeared to be. One end was wider than the other and seemed to be sealed with glossy black glass. The other end was clear, and Gwen lifted it to her eye. 'I think it's a kaleidoscope.'

'Be careful with that,' the pawnbroker said. 'That's going for seventy-five quid, and I've only just polished it.'

'Maybe that was what activated it.' Owen spoke quietly. 'He must have touched something accidentally and we picked up the signal.'

Gwen peered through the instrument at the room around her. The only difference she could see was that through the machine it seemed slightly darker. She tried to twist the other end, but it wouldn't budge. 'Maybe it's not a…'

She turned, the gadget still pressed to her eye, away from the dark shadow that was the doorway and faced Toshiko. 'Whoa!'

As her sight fell on the other woman, the view burst into an array of colour, yellows and reds glittering against golds and silvers. 'This is amazing.' As the image settled, Toshiko came back into view, a silver aura floating around her like mercury and blocking out the dull surrounds of the bland shop. Gwen stared. It was Tosh, but not Tosh. Her chin jutted defiantly upwards and her eyes glinted right into Gwen's own. Her dark hair blew back into the strange metallic background is if a breeze ran through the tube, and her skin shone with life and light. Gwen was still staring as Owen tugged the machine out of her grasp.

'Let's have a look.' He held it to his eye and gazed straight at Toshiko. 'Wow.' He paused. 'You look brilliant.'

Gwen blinked, readjusting to the ordinary light. Toshiko just looked awkward as far as she could see.

'Perhaps you shouldn't…' Toshiko let the sentence fade as Owen tilted his head, running his view through the kaleidoscope up and down her body.

'You look gorgeous.'

'Oh for God's sake, Owen!' Toshiko pulled the kaleidoscope away from him, but not before Gwen saw the faint blush creep onto the high spots of her cheeks. 'I don't think we should be playing with it.'

Owen squinted for a second and then disappointment etched slightly across his eyes as he looked at Toshiko. 'All right, all right.' He sniffed. 'But since you're in charge, you can pay the man for it.'

With the transaction complete and the alien technology

stowed in Toshiko's bag, they stepped back out onto the grimy streets of the estate.

'What's it made of?' Owen asked. 'It felt like metal.'

'The scanner couldn't identify it. Metal of some kind, but its denser than anything found on Earth. We'll have to wait until we get back to the Hub and run some proper—'

Toshiko's sentence went unfinished, the air knocked from her lungs as a group of boys burst through the middle of the three Torchwood operatives, yelling loudly as they ran. Gwen was flung against the side of the SUV, while Toshiko scrabbled at the floor, desperate to keep herself upright, with more success than Owen.

'My bag! They've got my bag!'

Gwen pushed herself away from the car and sprinted after the boys that ran and whooped ahead of them. 'I'm on it!'

Her feet thumped the pavement, scanning the youths to try and spot the one with the bag. They were a blur of trainers and baggy jackets. Which one had it? The group split and peeled off as they headed into the housing estate. Damn it, they'd never find them in there.

'The one on the left.' A dark-haired figure lunged ahead of her. 'That bastard's mine. He knocked me over.' Toshiko seemed barely out of breath as she ran, and, as Gwen watched her disappear round the corner, she almost stumbled. Toshiko Sato was outrunning her? That wasn't possible. She pushed herself forward.

As it was, the youths lost them in the warren of houses and tower blocks and the three regrouped, panting and sweating, at the SUV.

'Well, that's a good start,' Owen finally said. 'We find some alien technology and lose it again, all within twenty minutes.' He stretched slightly against the car, getting his breath back. 'Good work, Tosh.'

'Oh, get over yourself, Owen.' Toshiko flicked her hair over one shoulder and glared at the dark-haired man. 'And get in the car. We need to get back to the Hub and feed in the data from the handheld.' She tugged at the passenger door. 'We may not have it, but we can still figure out what it is and whether it's going to do any damage. We'll get it back.' She looked at both Gwen and Owen, both still red-faced from the chase. 'What are you waiting for?'

Gwen glanced over at Owen and saw her own surprise reflected on his face. Maybe Toshiko had found her leadership mojo after all.

'Not a lot here,' Jude sniffed as he rummaged through the contents.

He was right, Luke thought, rifling through the small purse. A single twenty pound note and a few coins. There wasn't even a credit card or two that they could have fun with for the afternoon before the woman cancelled it. He'd give the lipstick to his mum and Jude could have the tissues to blow his constantly running nose with.

'At least the bag looks like real leather. Someone might give us a fiver for it.'

'What's that?' The timid voice cut through the older boys' deeper growls.

Luke Parry hadn't even noticed that Danny Dillard was in

the Community Centre pool room. No one had actually used the building for years apart from the junkies that came in to settle down and shoot up most evenings, and the broken needles left scattered around stopped the young mums from using the place as a nursery. As did the words scrawled on the outside walls and the cracked and broken windows that the council seemed loath to replace. Luke and his crew didn't mind though. It gave them somewhere of their own when they needed it.

'What you doing here?' He let a little snarl creep into his voice, but he didn't mean it.

Fourteen-year-old Danny Dillard was harmless. If anything, Luke felt a bit sorry for him; not that he'd ever admit it. Even on the estate, where no one's life was easy, Danny's was pretty grim. His mum had run off when he was just a kid and left him in the hands of his dad. Luke's old man had been in the nick three times during his own seventeen years of living, but he wouldn't swap him for Steve Dillard. Not in a million years. Steve Dillard was a drunk with a mean reputation across the estate and beyond. It was usual to see both little Danny and his mum with dark bruises on their faces and arms, and in recent years Danny had been left to take both shares.

'Just reading my comic.' The skinny kid shrugged. His T-shirt was too big for him and probably donated by some charity or other at the school. 'What's that?' he asked again and nodded at the brown cylinder that had rolled slightly away.

'Dunno,' Luke answered. 'Just know it's bloody heavy.

Made me think there was something worth having in the stupid cow's bag.'

'Must be what she got in the pawnshop,' Jude said.

'Then it's no use to us.' Mickey chimed in, from where he sat against the wall, rolling a joint. 'He'll know we nicked it off them if we try and get a few quid off him for it.'

Luke picked it up. Mickey was right. Even if they could sell the thing, they'd have to take it off the estate and probably only get a tenner or so for it. He looked up at Danny. 'You want it?'

Danny's eyes widened. 'You mean it?'

'Sure.' Luke kept his voice bored. It wouldn't do for the others to see that he felt good about making the kid happy. 'Just don't let your dad get hold of it.'

A small shadow crossed the other boy's face as he carefully took the object. 'I won't.'

'Now clear off, and take your stupid comic with you.'

'Thanks, Luke. Thanks a lot.' Danny scuttled back to the corner he'd been occupying and grabbed his cheap anorak and comic, before disappearing out into the chilly grey air.

Jude sniffed. Mickey clicked his lighter. They both stared.

'What?' Luke looked from one to the other. 'We don't want it, do we?'

Mickey sucked his teeth. Jude swallowed a grin. But neither of them challenged him. Mickey took a long toke on the joint and passed it across. It was good, strong weed, and within minutes Danny Dillard and the strange object were both forgotten.

***

His dad was asleep when Danny quietly let himself into their small flat high up in one of the tatty blocks. He could hear the thick rattle of his snore, interspersed with wet breaths that Danny knew would stink of sour booze. The door clicked behind him and his nose wrinkled in the stale air that smelt vaguely of rancid milk. Danny did his best to keep the place clean but, between school and trying not to irritate his dad, it was difficult. He carefully pushed the door to the sitting room open and peered in. Horses raced on the old TV in the corner but the betting slip his dad must have been holding had dropped to the floor by the armchair as he'd fallen asleep.

Danny's insides shook a little. It probably meant whatever race his dad had bet on, he hadn't won. Empty lager cans littered the worn carpet and the ashtray on the small side table overflowed. When his dad woke up, he was going to have a headache. And if he hadn't won anything at the bookies, then it was likely that he wasn't going to have any money to go out drinking again. Without even realising he was doing it, Danny pressed himself back against the wall. He could see the night stretching out in front of him; at best, his dad would sleep until they were well into the evening, but if not there was no way Danny could hide in his room from his dad's bad mood for ever. Steve Dillard wasn't the kind of man who liked to deal with his anger himself. He liked to have someone to take it out on. Ghosts of old bruises whispered across his skin and his bones ached. In his head, his dad's shouting was just a sheet of angry noise and terror. Some things you just never got used to. He pulled the door to and crept away.

In his bedroom he opened a window to let in some cool, fresh air and carefully unwrapped the object from his coat. His half-read comic was forgotten. As soon as he'd seen the thing roll away from Luke Perry, he'd known he wanted it. They hadn't known what it was, but he had. It was a kaleidoscope, he was sure of it. He'd had a cheap one for Christmas from his nan back when his mum was still around. He'd loved the patterns it made as the beads inside shifted and turned. It was like looking into another magical world.

He lifted the long cylinder. It was cool and heavy in his hands. This one wouldn't break as easily as the last. No size ten shoe would be able to shatter it in one drunken stamp and leave it in glittering shards, its magic ruined, crushed into the carpet. This one might break the foot instead. He smiled a little but there was no warmth in it. That was something he'd like to see. A look of surprise in his dad's eyes that something was fighting back. Something wasn't breakable.

One end was black as marble and he peered through the other. His room grew gloomy. This wasn't like his old kaleidoscope. That was all patterns and colours; he hadn't been able to see anything real through it. He tried turning the far section but nothing happened. He frowned, his heart dragging itself back down to the dark place it hid in. For a brief moment, he'd thought he had something special. Something of his own. He chewed his bottom lip. Maybe it wasn't a traditional toy, but it had to do something. He could hear his dad still snoring, and it had the deep, steady rhythm of someone who wouldn't be woken easily. Danny had learned to gauge those sounds over the years. It was always a risky bet, because the only things predictable about Steve Dillard were his drinking and his temper, but Danny was pretty sure he could go back into the lounge without disturbing the monster from its slumber. He made his way back, the heavy tube at his side. Maybe if he looked at the TV with it, it would do something. From a safe place in the doorway, he tried. The horses still ran as normal round the track but, instead of the bright green of the turf, the background had deadened to a midnight blue. His heart sank further. Whatever this thing did, he wasn't sure he could figure it out.

His dad snorted, a low cough of saliva and snot perhaps stuck momentarily in his throat, and Danny jumped, instinctively turning to look at him, the machine still pressed to his eye. Steve Dillard settled back into his sleep.

Danny Dillard gasped. The view had come alive in silvers and golds. His dad's skin shone. The stained and old flowery armchair that had once been his mum's favourite was lost in a metallic ocean that hummed with a sheen of pearlescent blues and pinks, but his father's image was clear. And it was *clean*. Frowning, he lowered the kaleidoscope or whatever it was for a moment. He looked at his father.

Steve Dillard wasn't much more than 40 but, with his diet of beer, cigarettes and cheap takeaway food, his body had long ago given up any attempt at holding itself together and had slumped outwards in a large, pale belly that was often found hanging below his T-shirts. His skin was dry and blotchy on his face, and his smile was seen so rarely that his

84

mouth had thinned. He looked like a man in his fifties easily; a properly old man, rather than someone's dad.

Danny raised the kaleidoscope again and looked carefully. The glory of the background was distracting but he focused on his father instead. Through the glass, his dad's skin seemed to have smoothed out. The lines that had set into his forehead from his permanent frown had disappeared. Instead of looking like a drunk asleep, his dad just looked like anyone else having a quick afternoon nap in front of the telly. Danny smiled. His fingers tingled as the kaleidoscope grew warm under them. It tickled. The heat spread through him and his heart lifted a little. This was a good thing. He could tell.

'So, you had it. And then you lost it?' Ianto looked doubtfully from Toshiko back to Gwen and Owen.

'Something like that,' Gwen muttered.

'Stop stressing.' Toshiko flicked her hair back over her shoulder. 'We'll find it again. You're always so uptight.'

Gwen's hand paused on the way to sip her coffee. Had Tosh really just said that? Her eyes caught Ianto's and they both raised an eyebrow.

'You feeling all right, Tosh?' Owen frowned.

'Yes. Why?' She ushered Ianto away from the main computer and confidently took his place at the console.

'You just seem a little… different, that's all. I can't put my finger on it.'

'Well, if you don't know what you're trying to say, Dr Harper,' Toshiko muttered, focused on the screen. 'Then don't say anything at all.' She flashed him a short, hard smile. 'It's a waste of all our time.'

Owen's mouth dropped slightly, and Gwen held back a short giggle. Even she had to admit what she was seeing on Owen's face. This new attitude Toshiko Sato had adopted was kind of sexy. The only person that didn't seem amused was Ianto, who looked from Toshiko to Owen and then back again.

'Whatever you say, boss,' Owen said, and then shivered suddenly. 'That running's given me the jitters. Anyone got any chocolate?'

'No, but I'll go and get some.' Gwen's stomach gurgled. She was feeling a little in need of a sugar rush herself.

Danny watched his dad for hours while he slept. He watched him until his arms were cramped from holding the heavy object to his eye, even though he'd been resting them on his knees ever since he'd slid down to the floor to watch his dad more comfortably. His face ached from squinting through the small lens. His body hummed from the heat coming from the kaleidoscope. Through it, his dad had slowly changed as the hours and minutes had ticked by. Not only had the frown lines disappeared but there was a small smile playing on his mouth, and Danny was pretty sure his dad's thinning hair had thickened and the heavy paunch that hung over the rim of his cheap trousers had somehow diminished. Danny was fascinated by it. His heart thumped loudly in his chest. He couldn't stop watching. His dad almost looked like a dad.

Eventually, as the day outside sank into the cool grip of

the evening, his fingers cramped and he slowly lowered the instrument. His muscles screamed with the action, hot white pain shooting through his young joints. He blinked. How long had he been there? His eyes burned as they adjusted to the gloom. He pulled himself slowly to his feet, pins and needles cramping his feet. He shivered and took two careful steps forward. Was it his imagination or had his dad's snore become softer? Did he really look just a little bit thinner? Danny rubbed his aching head. He was suddenly starving, but he didn't know what for. The warmth that had flooded his thin system slipped away, and he trembled. He needed a jumper. And some food. And soon his dad would wake up.

He found a solitary two-finger chocolate bar in the back of the fridge behind the six-pack of cheap beers, and he ate it quickly before scurrying back to his room. He hid the kaleidoscope under his pillow and tried to concentrate on his homework, but his eyes kept shutting as they scanned the textbooks and his fingers were numb and cramped. His mind drifted. He just wanted to get the strange toy out and look through it again. Even under his jumper, goose bumps trickled across his arms.

After half an hour, his blood stilled as footsteps thudded heavily along the short corridor. His heart beat in time with them. A door closed. A few seconds later the toilet flushed. Danny's eyes widened. The footsteps came closer and his bedroom door pushed open. A large shadow fell across the carpet. Danny swallowed.

His dad looked at him from the doorway and frowned, still looking half-asleep.

'What you doing?' The words came out in a grunt.

'Homework,' Danny whispered, softly. This was the worst time, when his dad had just woken up. This was the danger time. The wrong word could set him off. The chocolate curdled in his empty stomach. There was a long pause.

'Good.' His dad mumbled, before scratching his tummy and turning away. 'Good.'

Danny sat frozen until he heard the front door click shut. He stared at the wall. Where had his dad gone? Back to the pub? Normally he'd yell or shout or growl before storming out, especially if he had a hangover. Normally Danny would be 'just like his mother' or 'just another waste of space kid filling up the world'. Normally things were louder in the flat. His heart was only just returning to its own hesitant rhythm when the door clicked shut again. Barely ten minutes had passed.

'Danny?' His dad's voice carried easily through the flat. The boy's stomach turned to water. 'Danny, come out here!'

For a second Danny just licked his lips nervously and then slowly pushed the unread homework aside. If he made his dad come in to get him it would be worse, whatever 'it' was going to be tonight. He was still sore from his hours crouched down in the sitting room and the tension that crept out from his heart and stomach made his muscles ache worse. He hoped his dad didn't hit him tonight. Shouting he could manage, but his thin body wasn't up for more bruises.

Something in the kitchen smelt good; hot and warm and appetising.

'Hurry up,' his dad grunted. 'It'll get cold.'

Two plates sat on the kitchen side, the brown paper parcels opened up to reveal thickly battered fish and a large portion of golden chips. Danny's mouth watered.

'Got you some peas, too.' His dad nodded in the direction of a small polystyrene tub. 'You don't eat enough veg.' Steve Dillard picked up his plate and headed towards the sitting room. 'You coming?'

Danny nodded silently before picking up the heavy plate and the ketchup bottle. They ate quietly in front of the soaps on the telly until both their plates were cleared. Danny got up to take them into kitchen and his dad smiled.

'Good lad.'

As he washed the dishes, he heard the click of his dad's lighter and a small chuckle at something on the screen. The food had tasted good, but his small stomach wasn't used to eating so much, and the grease and the nervous tension were combining to make him feel sick. What had happened to his dad? Why was he in such a good mood?

Back in his room, Danny fiddled with his homework for another hour or so and then crept into bed. The kaleidoscope was hard under his thin pillow. His skin itched to hold it again and feel the warmth that flooded him as he'd watched his dad sleep. He flicked out the small lamp and plunged the room into darkness. He slid one hand under the pillow and touched the strange toy. He liked the feel of it and couldn't help but wonder if maybe it was like some kind of magic wand. He'd looked through it, and now his dad was acting different. Better different. Could that be it, or was it just crazy? He blinked the time away, his head in a whirl, until he heard the TV fall silent and his dad's heavy tread in the corridor. A head peered round his door for a moment and Danny squeezed his eyes tight until the room was once more back in darkness.

He waited a full half-hour until he was pretty sure his dad was asleep, before pulling the kaleidoscope out from under his pillow and padding towards his dad's bedroom and pushing the door open ever so slightly. His father's large body was a mound under the duvet, but his arms and head were free from the covers and he breathed deeply and evenly. Danny crept inside, pressing himself against the long radiator. With aching arms, he lifted the object and peered through, willing it to do its magic some more. As he lost himself in the silvers and the glowing skin of his father, he sighed and welcomed the warmth.

'Are those all yours?' Ianto looked at the pile of chocolate wrappers scattered across the small area of workstation that Gwen was occupying. 'I'm surprised you're not the size of a house.'

He had a point, Gwen realised, as she surveyed the mess. She'd eaten at least five bars while she'd been trawling through the database without even really noticing. Her teeth and tongue felt coated in sweetness and she needed a coffee. She glanced over to where Owen sat reading the paper on the small sofa against the wall.

'Looks like I'm not the only one.' A small pile of ripped-up brightly coloured paper littered the floor by his feet. She was mildly surprised. She couldn't even remember picking up that many bars when she'd run to the shop. It wasn't like her at all.

'Put the newspaper down, Owen.' Toshiko didn't even turn away from her computer screen. 'I can always find you something to do.'

'There is such a thing as a lunch break, you know.' Owen peered up over the sports pages. 'I think it's the law. And given that it's now gone eleven at night, I think I'm entitled to one, don't you?'

'There are no entitlements in Torchwood. If you're looking for perks, go back to the NHS.'

Owen crumpled the paper up, but got to his feet. 'I think this power trip's gone to your head.'

Ianto frowned. 'Maybe he's got a point.'

'What do you mean?' Gwen scooped up the rubbish and tossed it into the small bin under the desk.

'Doesn't Tosh seem different to you? Way more confident than normal?' Ianto sipped his coffee thoughtfully. 'She never speaks to anyone like she has today. I haven't even heard her say "please" since she got back.' He looked at Gwen. 'Did anything happen when you were out there before the alien technology was stolen?'

Gwen shrugged. 'No, not really. We got to the estate and found the pawnbroker's shop. I had a play with the thing though. Just looked through it for a few seconds, and then Owen did the same. We paid for it and left and then the kids ran through us and stole it.'

'You and Owen looked through it?'

Gwen nodded.

'What did you look at?'

'Tosh.' She frowned and looked over at Toshiko. 'We both looked at Tosh…'

'And now she's different,' Ianto muttered.

'OK, I think I've found something that fits our description.' Toshiko looked up. 'Come and see.'

On the large screen an object rotated. It was almost identical to the one they'd seen at the shop, cylindrical in shape and with one clear end and one blackened.

'It's a Rehabilitator.'

'A what?' Owen peered in.

Toshiko clicked another button and quickly scanned the information. 'Jack wrote a report on one of them, back in the nineties. Apparently, there are quite a few of them scattered across the galaxy. They're the relics of an old alien civilisation that used them to maintain civil harmony. They were found by another humanoid race who colonised this dead planet and then they found the devices had peculiar properties and installed them in prisons. If a person is viewed through one, they become the ideal version of themselves according to the viewer's concept of ideal. For a transition to be completely effective the candidate must be viewed for several hours, and then they emerge a newer, better person.'

'Sounds a little too good to be true.' Gwen raised an eyebrow.

'And you'd be right. It was. The whole society was sent into disarray when three of the Rehabilitators were stolen and used by some sort of terrorist group to turn ordinary law-abiding citizens into killers and assassins. They fell out of use after that and, other than a few turning up here and there, there's nothing more to tell about them.'

'What's that box thing?' Ianto pointed at a second image in the corner of the screen.

'That's the viewing box. The alloy the machine is made out of emits tiny particles into the skin when pressed into it like you would do if you held it to the soft tissue around your eye. They create a pleasant but highly addictive sensation. When the Rehabilitator is placed inside, it creates a very thin but dense barrier between the person and the object. Close enough for the device to be activated by the proximity of the eye, but totally prevents contact with the skin.'

'Well, that explains a lot of things.' Ianto folded his arms.

'What do you mean?'

'I think I get his point.' Gwen looked at Toshiko. 'He tried to make it a minute ago. Tosh, you've been really different since we found that device earlier. It must be because me and Owen both looked at you through it.'

'Don't be so ridiculous.' Toshiko's eyes seemed less certain than her voice. 'You only looked through it for a couple of seconds.'

'I know. But we still did it. And you're still different.'

'And I'm still craving something,' Owen added. 'Even after all that chocolate.'

Gwen knew what he meant. There was just the tiniest itch under her skin and she couldn't figure out how to scratch it.

The image on the screen changed, one window closing as the computers prioritised what the team needed to see. Toshiko smiled. 'There you go. We've got another energy burst on the estate. Same as before. She looked triumphantly at Ianto. 'I told you we'd find it again soon enough. Sometimes you're so anal.' She laughed a little at her own joke and then led the way to the lift.

Gwen watched her go, her mouth not dropped open like the two boys' had, but still more than a little shocked. What had they done to shy, sweet Toshiko? Gwen could remember thinking that the other woman needed some more confidence not long before looking through the Rehabilitator. The sassy and sexy new attitude must have been provided by whatever Owen had been thinking. Bloody Owen Harper. Sex was never far from his thoughts. She watched the swing of Toshiko Sato's hips as she strode towards the exit. The change in her had been fun to watch for a while, but knowing it had been brought on by alien technology was just disconcerting. When the bloody hell was the old Tosh going to resurface?

'Come on,' she told Owen. 'You and me had better go with her. We created this monster. We'd better manage her.'

Owen nodded, and Gwen saw an echo of something dark in his eyes as he nodded. For a moment all her irritation at him dissipated as she realised why he'd been such a pain over the leadership issue. She'd been too blinded by her own sense of loss over Jack to really think about how Owen was feeling. The doctor needed to prove himself again. Even though they'd all played their part in the End of Days, it was Owen who'd led the way, and it was Owen who'd shot Jack. And now he'd be feeling more guilt at his part in these changes in Toshiko. Under all the angst in their relationship, Gwen felt for him. That kind of weight would be hard on the soul.

She wanted to squeeze his arm and tell him it would all be OK in time, but she figured he'd have to get there himself and, ironically, they had no time for it now. Instead, she just grinned. 'Race you to the lift.'

'I'll just stay here then, shall I?' Ianto called after them.

'Get some coffee on and order a pizza.' Gwen winked as she stepped into the lift. 'We won't be long.'

The first sign of a change came when they stepped out of the SUV and onto the pavement. Gwen spotted it in the slight slump of Toshiko's shoulders and the hesitant nibble at her bottom lip as she peered both ways in the gloom.

'You all right, Tosh?' Gwen asked quietly.

'Yes. Gosh yes, sorry. Just felt a little strange.' She glanced at the handheld monitor. 'I think the device is in that block there.' Her eyes flickered forward and then down again, seeking reassurance in the metal.

'Let's go then.' Gwen jogged ahead, the other two behind her. Toshiko didn't overtake or even come level. Whatever the Kaleidoscope had done to her it looked like it was wearing off, which in some ways would be a relief, but the technology-altered Tosh had at least taken on the role of leader with relish. How would she cope now?

It was late, but there was plenty of activity around the estate. A group of teenage boys hung out in the central play area designed for those much younger than themselves, laughing and smoking on the swings. Their conversation died slightly as they watched the three strangers go past. Gwen wondered if it was the same gang that had robbed them this morning, but in the gloom she couldn't make them out and, anyway, she wasn't here to make an arrest.

Music blared from somewhere above as they paused at the entrance to the central block.

'What floor?' Owen asked.

'Can't be sure. The reading's not that precise.' Toshiko stared at the machine. 'I think it's somewhere near the top.'

'Let's take the stairs then.' Only one bulb was working on the ground floor and a vague smell of damp and stale urine drifted towards them from the dark shadows.

'Do we have to?' Toshiko asked. 'Can't we just take the lift?'

'And stop at every floor to see if it's the right one? Have you ever been in one of these lifts? We'll kill it.'

'She's right.' Owen followed Gwen up the first flight. 'I don't know about you, but I don't fancy being stuck in a lift on this estate. It'd be weeks before anyone found us.'

'Well OK. If you both think we should.' Toshiko started to climb.

By the time they were stood outside the right flat, they were all out of breath.

'Is it just me, or have we done our exercise quota for the day?' Owen leant against the wall. 'That sprint this morning was enough for me.'

'You're getting old.' Gwen smiled, before glancing back at Toshiko. 'This the one?'

Toshiko checked the readout. 'Yes. It's here, and it's active.'

Gwen banged on the door. She did it hard and fast and with the confidence that only the police would use when waking up strangers in the middle of the night. It was a specific kind of thump that demanded an immediate response. She repeated it until eventually the door opened.

A small boy stared blearily back at them. He wasn't one of the youths that had robbed them that afternoon; that much was obvious straight away. This child was a good four or five years younger than any of those had been and he was short and skinny. They'd have caught this boy without a problem.

'Look,' Toshiko whispered.

Gwen had already spotted it. The Rehabilitator hung at the boy's side.

'Hello.' Gwen smiled. 'What's your name?'

'Danny,' he answered quietly.

'What's going on?' A man shuffled into view out of the gloom and flicked a light on. He looked half-asleep, his dressing gown barely pulled across his naked chest. He placed one arm protectively around the boy's shoulders.

'Are you Danny's dad?' Gwen asked.

'Yeah, I'm Steve Dillard. Anything wrong? Is Danny in trouble?' His concern wasn't what Gwen had expected, given how untidy the flat looked from her position on the doorstep. Everything was coated in grime and dust gathered at the edges of the tatty carpet.

'Can we come inside?'

'Who are you?'

'Torchwood. A government agency.'

'Never heard of you.' Mr Dillard still stepped aside, and

Gwen led the other two inside, before following the boy's father into the sitting room. From the corner of her eye, she saw Toshiko's nose wrinkle slightly. If a seat was offered, Gwen bet that none of them would take it. She felt sorry for the poor kid, standing between them with big wide eyes that she thought had probably been scared for as long as he could remember. She'd seen that look a few times over the years. This was a kid that fell just under the radar of social security; abused just a bit, but not badly enough to be taken away. He might not get fed enough, but he got fed sometimes, just in the same way as he might not get beaten all the time, but he definitely did sometimes. It looked to Gwen that little Danny Dillard was a boy who had no idea what it was like to be truly loved.

'Where did you get that, Danny?'

The boy looked from Gwen to his dad and back again.

'You're not in trouble.' Toshiko smiled. 'Honestly.'

He shrugged. 'Some of the older boys gave it to me. They didn't want it.'

'What is it, Danny?' His dad frowned as he looked at what his son was holding. 'When did you get that?' He paused. 'You shouldn't be hanging around with those kids. They're trouble.'

'I wasn't. I was just reading my comic,' Danny whispered.

'Make sure it stays that way. You're clever, Danny. You're better than them.'

The boy stared at his dad as if he was a stranger, and Gwen felt a trickle of realisation. It was the middle of the night and the boy had answered the door with the Rehabilitator in his hand. She knew how dull ordinary things looked through it, certainly not interesting enough to keep a young boy up. There was only one person in the flat Danny Dillard could have been watching through it: his dad. How long had he been doing it? How different was the Steve Dillard of tonight compared with the Steve Dillard that had got up that morning?

'We need to take that machine back with us. Sorry.' Gwen held her hand out. 'It's stolen government property.' She smiled softly and very slowly Danny held out his arm. He looked like he might cry.

'It's very heavy. Be careful with it.'

'Thank you.' Gwen took it from him and tucked it into the inside of her jacket.

'What on Earth is it?' Mr Dillard frowned.

'Nothing very exciting.' Owen stepped forward. 'But unfortunately we have reason to believe it may be mildly radioactive.'

'What? But—'

'It's really nothing for you to worry about. I've got a pill here for each of you to take that will completely wipe out any negative effects your systems may be undergoing.' He tugged a small container from his pocket. 'Now, if you could just get you and Danny here a glass of water? We need to see you take these for the sake of paperwork.' He smiled.

Within a few minutes, both the father and son were asleep and the team had got them back into their beds. By the morning, the Retcon would have done its job and all memory of Torchwood and the Rehabilitator would be gone. Sometimes Gwen found it strange to wonder how many people were wandering around Cardiff thinking that nothing extraordinary had ever happened in their lives and all because of that magic little pill. Maybe one day she'd be one of them. The thought made her shiver. The other two were obviously having similar thoughts, because for a few minutes the atmosphere in the SUV was as dark as the night outside.

'Come on,' Gwen said softly. 'Let's get this thing stored away back at the Hub and then maybe we can all go home and get some sleep.'

For once, Owen did as he was told.

It was a fortnight later when Ianto found Gwen staring at the Rehabilitator, a frown eating into her pretty face.

'What's up? I thought we were done with that.'

'I keep thinking about chocolate,' she muttered.

'I'm not with you.'

'The amount of chocolate me and Owen ate that day when we'd looked at Tosh through this thing.'

'What about it? We know the Rehabilitator is addictive, it said so on all that information Tosh found.'

Gwen looked up. 'That's my problem.' She clicked on the intercom through to the main area of the Hub. 'Owen?'

'Yep.' His voice had an edge of metal.

'Addiction. Is it a physical or a mental thing?'

'Could be either or, depending on the addiction. Why?'

'That kid that had the Rehabilitator is bugging me. I keep

thinking about all that crap we ate that day.'

There was a pause as Owen thought this through.

'Oh. I see where you're coming from,' he said at last. 'The Retcon cleared his memory, but if this thing had a hold on his system…' The sentence faded. 'Shit.'

'We need to check on him. Where's Tosh?'

'I'm here.' Toshiko came in. 'I heard.'

'Me and Owen will go and check him out. You and Ianto may as well stay here.'

'Will do.'

Toshiko was perfectly capable in the field and had proven her bravery on lots of occasions since Gwen had met her, but she was happiest amidst the technology in the Hub. Gwen and Owen were the natural field agents and always had been.

Gwen noticed the change in the flat before they'd even got inside. The door was covered in a new blue gloss coating and a small pot plant sat outside the door. She raised an eyebrow at Owen. Toshiko had been back to her normal self ever since they'd got the artefact back, but it looked like Danny Dillard's work had had more lasting results.

'Yes?' Steve Dillard opened the door. He stared at them for a second and then, before Gwen could speak, his eyes blurred with hope and dread. 'Have you got news about Danny?'

Gwen glanced at Owen, and they stepped inside. The flat was clean and fresh, the dirt they'd seen two weeks previously had been stripped away, and it looked like Mr Dillard himself had lost weight. Gwen had been pretty sure that he'd been missing a side tooth when they'd spoken last, but now he had a full set. Just how many changes was that piece of technology able to bring about in a person? How much would Toshiko have changed if they'd kept on looking?

'News?' Owen asked carefully.

'Yes, he's been missing three days now.' Steve Dillard paced slightly. 'You are the police, aren't you?'

Gwen ducked the question. 'We just need you to go over the events leading up to Danny's disappearance for us again.' Her heart thumped. Danny was gone.

'He didn't disappear. He ran away.' His voice dripped with pain. 'And I don't know why. Things have been good.' He stared out of the window. 'It started about two weeks ago. He got moody; bit withdrawn. I thought it was just teenage stuff or something at school, but he wouldn't talk about it. To be honest, I've been a bit fuzzy myself lately. It's only been the past week or so that I seem to have sharpened up... and then this happens. Anyway, he was staying up late and saying he couldn't sleep and eating loads of sweets and chocolates. I think he was stealing them.'

He sighed.

'Three days ago, I came home and he was gone. And so was his backpack and some of his clothes. I started a new job last week, so I hadn't been around to check on him, but I know he ran away. He took fifty quid from the jar in the kitchen.' Steve Dillard's voice broke. 'And that worries me, because he won't get very far on fifty quid. What will happen to him then?'

'I'm sorry,' Gwen whispered. 'I'm so sorry.'

'We'll do our best to find him,' Owen added.

'But what will happen to him if he doesn't come home?' the man repeated plaintively.

A small part of Gwen's heart tore away and burned in the man's obvious pain. This was her fault. It was their fault. They hadn't thought the whole thing through properly and had just smugly gone after the artefact rather than thinking through the human effect. Jack wouldn't have done that, she thought sadly. But Jack Harkness had just left them to it.

When they let themselves out, Steve Dillard was quietly crying, his hands gripping the top of the radiator for support. Gwen's mouth tasted sour, and she wasn't sure if it was her own guilt at not thinking through the effects of the Rehabilitator when it mattered, or whether it was just being in the presence of the man's grief. Perhaps it was a bit of both. Maybe this was why Jack Harkness sometimes hid dark clouds behind his dazzling smile. There was so much to carry inside when you worked for Torchwood.

'Do you think we'll find him?' Owen asked quietly.

'I doubt it.' Gwen peered out over Cardiff from the height of the tower block. It was a big city and easy for a kid to get lost in. And that was if Danny hadn't got on a train and taken himself to a bigger city like London. Her heart felt heavy and she longed for Jack. 'We'll try, though.'

They were still quiet when they got back to the Hub. Ianto and Toshiko were in the Boardroom, and the smell of fresh coffee wafted out towards them. Gwen was just about to reach for her own white with two sugars when Toshiko stopped her.

'Not so fast.'

'What do you mean?' Gwen frowned.

'This is your coffee.'

Ianto moved out of the way, and Toshiko picked up a separate mug that sat on the side. She held it out towards Gwen. It was hot, black and looked strong.

'I thought we'd established that it isn't.'

Toshiko shrugged. 'Rules can be changed. This is your coffee, and we all know it.'

Gwen peered over at Owen, and he smiled.

'It's yours. Take it.'

A short alarm buzzed out and four sets of groans and expletives bounced off the walls. Something was coming through the Rift again, and coffee was just going to have to wait.

Danny sat curled up against the wall, the bare floorboards underneath him making his skinny body ache. Still, not for much longer. On the other side of the room, three teenagers with long dreads passed a bong around, each sucking in deep lungfuls of mellow smoke. He was lucky they'd let him in. He peered down at his own small set of equipment. The spoon, the lighter, the belt and the syringe. For a moment hot breath raced in his ear but he gritted his teeth and crushed the memory of what he'd done to earn it.

At least here he could get what he needed easily enough and there were more ways of getting it. His dad seemed like a long way away, further than six months and more distant than a couple of miles. Sometimes his old life seemed just like someone else's memory or a vague dream, half-remembered.

With shaking hands, he prepared the syringe and greedily injected. A memory itched at the back of his head of something more beautiful, but he couldn't quite reach it. At least when he was high that awful sensation faded. He smiled and leaned back.

Behind his eyes, silvers and golds swirled and warmth flooded his body.

The Wrong Hands

ANDREW CARTMEL

'There's nothing quite like starting the day with a cauterised cadaver,' said Jack jauntily.

His words echoed, sounding a little hollow in the tiled room. The police morgue was a cold, bleach-scented place, although 'cold' didn't quite do it justice. There was a *chill* that crept into your bones. Gwen always felt it, standing in one of these places, looking down at the dead.

In this case, she was looking at the grisly remains of a young man – a teenager in fact – and they were grisly chiefly because they were in two separate pieces, occupying two separate tables, a rare privilege here, where space was always at a premium.

Gwen swallowed. Her throat was a little dry thanks to the aggressive air conditioning in the room. She forced herself to look with detachment. The body had been divided fairly neatly at the waist. And, as Jack had just remarked, the wound had been tidily cauterised.

Gwen made sure her voice was steady and detached and professional. 'What was his name?'

'Rhett Seyers. Eighteen years old. Drug dealer. They start them early on the Machen estate.'

'The Machen? I know it,' said Gwen. 'You have to watch your back around there, I can tell you.'

'Even the police?'

'Especially the police.'

'You were so cute in that uniform,' said Jack. 'Size nines and a stab vest.'

'My feet are not size nines,' said Gwen curtly.

'He was selling crack, or "slinging rock", as I believe you young people say these days. I attribute this to the pernicious influence of American television. The terminology I mean, not the drug dealing.'

'So he was dealing on the Machen estate…'

'Well, on the car park of the supermarket across the road, actually. At least that was where the body was found. The body *parts*.'

Gwen steeled herself to look dispassionately once again at the divided corpse. Businesslike, that was the order of the day. 'So, what do you think did this to him?'

'If you're talking about the actual implement used, then it's definitely alien in origin.'

'How can you be sure?'

'The neatness of the job,' Jack told her. 'He was sliced in two with a single smooth blow. And the wound was heat-sealed, virtually instantly, so there was no blood. You all right?'

'Yes,' said Gwen. 'Fine.'

'At first the police thought he'd been killed somewhere

110

else and the body drained of blood and cut up before he was transported and dumped outside the Happy Price supermarket. A kind of Black Dahlia number. But with a gender flip. There was no trace of blood there in the car park, so the police assumed he must have been—'

'Killed elsewhere and transported there,' supplied Gwen.

'Right. But there was no blood for a completely different reason. The heat sealing. Boiled off any bodily fluids. Or solidified them. You know, sort of cooked or coagulated. You sure you're all right? Looking a bit green round the gills, there. Not that I'm saying you have gills. Unlike some I could name.'

Gwen forced a smile. 'No. I'm fine. Go on.'

'Well, that's about it, really. Like I say, alien weaponry of some kind. Nothing currently available on Earth would have made such a—'

'Don't say neat again.'

Jack nodded, as though acknowledging the reasonableness of this request. 'Such a *precise* job. No conventional contemporary human artefact could both cut and burn like that. So it has to be something else. Something from off-world.'

'Right. OK. Great. Is that all we know?'

'No.' Jack shook his head and walked over to a bench where surgical instruments gleamed in stainless-steel bowls. Propped between the bowls was a green rectangular plastic folder containing papers. Jack looked at the folder. 'No,' he repeated. 'We also know he's not the first.'

'There've been others?'

Jack tapped the folder with his fingernail. 'That's what Ianto seems to think. Isn't that right, Ianto?'

Gwen realised he was now addressing his communications earpiece. He had an annoying habit of doing this, entirely without warning, in the middle of a conversation with you.

'Yes,' said Ianto, his voice, responding to Jack's question, was suddenly also alive in her earpiece. Gwen pictured Ianto back at the Hub, ironic expression on his face, sitting in front of a computer, no doubt with a coffee. 'Judging by that autopsy report, this killing could be the same as at least two others.'

'Wonderful,' said Gwen.

'I'll need a tissue sample to be certain.' Ianto's voice was businesslike and matter-of-fact, but intimately close in her ear.

Gwen's eyes strayed again to what had once been Rhett Seyers.

As if reading her mind through the sheer proximity of the earpiece to her brain, Ianto's voice said, 'But none of them were cut in two like your victim, though they were apparently killed with the same device.'

'Or the same *kind* of device,' said Jack.

'You think there might be more than one?' Gwen saw the implication. 'More than one alien heat-weapon out there? Capable of this?'

'I've learned to be pessimistic,' said Jack.

'So we're looking for at least one person and possibly more running around the streets of Cardiff with this very dangerous alien weaponry.'

'Maybe not running,' said Jack, and smiled.

Gwen didn't smile back. She didn't think the situation was in any way funny.

Ianto's voice murmured in her ear, 'Your friend on the table there—'

'On two tables actually,' said Jack.

'Well, like him,' continued Ianto, 'the other two victims were also drug dealers.'

'So someone has somehow got hold of this alien weapon—'

'Or weapons,' said Jack.

'And they are going around with it, killing drug dealers.'

Jack gave a thoughtful shrug. 'Either that or we have an alien heat-gun complete with an alien gunman using it, and it's this alien who is specialising in bumping off drug dealers.'

Gwen looked at him. 'So, what are you suggesting? An alien vigilante?'

Jack smiled. 'Yeah. Possibly. We haven't had one of those for a while.'

'Or…' came Ianto's voice again.

Jack rolled his eyes at Gwen.

'… it could be black market,' Ianto went on. 'There's that group we've been trying to find for – what? – a couple of months now. Whoever they are, they've been selling stolen alien gear, making a fortune.'

'Could be,' agreed Jack. 'Good thinking, Ianto. See what you can find out.'

Ianto ended his transmission, and Gwen turned and

started for the door, expecting Jack to follow, eager to set off back to the Hub. For her own part, she was anxious to get out into the sunshine and the fresh air again.

But instead Jack lingered behind. 'Wait a minute,' he said.

Gwen paused in the doorway and looked back at him. He was standing by the bowls of surgical instruments, looking pensively at them.

'What for?' she said.

'Tissue sample.'

Gwen remembered. 'Oh Jesus, yes, that.'

As Jack sorted through the instruments, they rang in their steel bowls, incongruously musical in the cold tiled room.

It took half an hour in late-morning traffic to get back to the Hub and another full half an hour for Ianto to complete the comparison of the tissue sample. Although, to be fair, a considerable portion of that time was taken up by him wrestling with the coffee machine and seeking to achieve what he referred to as 'an acceptable *crema*' on his cappuccino.

On microscopic examination, the damage to the tissue sample Jack had collected proved identical to the damage on the samples taken from the two previous victims. 'The late Alex Brown and the late Bobby Pembroke,' said Ianto. He filed the microscope slides back in a refrigerated drawer and pushed it smoothly shut.

'And now Rhett Seyers.'

'The common denominator,' said Jack, 'is that they're all drug dealers.'

Ianto frowned. 'Bit young, aren't they?'

114

'Not even precocious by today's standards. Maybe the government is running some kind of fast-track scheme to get school leavers started selling crack cocaine.'

'Don't be so cynical,' said Gwen. 'It doesn't suit you. And you know they're dealers because…?'

'Police files,' said Jack. He was sitting with his feet up, folding a piece of paper. 'That's the only factor linking them all.' He finished folding the paper into the shape of a paper plane. 'Apart from the weapon that killed them.' He snapped his wrist and sent the plane sailing gracefully through the shadows of the Hub.

'Not the only factor,' said Gwen.

Jack took his eyes off the plane's trajectory and looked at her.

She tried to keep any hint of smugness out of her voice. 'The victims are also all linked by the Machen Estate.'

Ianto shook his head and turned back to the computer screen. 'No, sorry, but that's not right, Gwen. Yes, Rhett Seyers was found there. But Alex Brown was dumped in a recycling bin in the town centre, and Bobby Pembroke was fished out of the bay.'

'I didn't say that they were all *found* in the Machen Estate. I said they were all linked by it.' Gwen turned to her own computer screen where she had set up a virtual incident board, comprising the facts she'd pulled off various databases in the past half-hour. 'Alex Brown's last known address was on the Machen. Flat 5 in Pan House.'

'Pan?' said Jack, his forehead furrowing. 'Is that estate in any way connected with Arthur Machen?'

115

Gwen consulted her screen again. 'Arthur Machen, yes, right, that's the full, official name of the place. But everyone just calls it the Machen.'

'Why do you ask?' said Ianto, looking speculatively at Jack. 'Who was he?'

'Writer. Interesting guy.' Jack nodded thoughtfully, 'Aleister Crowley was a big fan of his. I knew him vaguely.'

'Crowley or Machen?' asked Gwen. She had heard of Aleister Crowley, at least.

'Arthur Machen,' said Jack. 'Him, I knew.'

'But only vaguely?' said Ianto.

'Well enough to feel sorry that he's had a dump like that named after him.' Jack stood behind Gwen and peered over her shoulder at the picture of the estate on her screen. 'Poor guy.'

'And the second dealer,' continued Gwen, rather annoyed that they'd got sidetracked before she'd finished presenting the facts she'd so painstakingly ferreted out. 'Bobby Pembroke, he also lived on the Machen, with his family. In Bowmen House.'

'Bowmen, yes,' said Jack. 'That makes sense. I think we better go to this place and have a sniff around.'

The Machen Estate consisted of five four-storey blocks, rectangular brown- and white-brick structures called Pan House, Pyramid House, Bowmen House, Jade House and Sangraal House. Seen in the aerial photo from Gwen's file they were arranged like a spread hand of cards on a casino table, oblongs stretching radially back from the shallow semicircle of the access road which ran from the west gate to the east gate of the estate.

These twin gates were ornate arches set in the long red-brick wall that separated them and screened the estate from the main road. But behind this handsome old wall, ornately scrolled and topped with grubby cream brickwork, there was a shadowy wasteland of dead grass, abandoned crisp packets, plastic cola bottles and beer tins.

In the middle of this patch of wasteland was what had once been a quaint little cottage pub. It was called the Red Hand. According to Jack, this unusual name, like the names of all the other buildings, was drawn from the literary works of Arthur Machen. Gwen had printed out a map of the place and she'd studied it, scrutinising the names, on the way here.

She walked past the west gate, along the street. Putting her map away and looking around she immediately spotted the gleaming black Torchwood SUV, parked opposite the Happy Price supermarket. The Happy Price was sited facing the east gate of the estate, as though to catch unwary inhabitants of the Machen as they emerged into the outside world.

Approaching from behind, Gwen could see the silhouette of Jack sitting in the SUV. She crossed the road, glancing automatically both ways for approaching cars, and hurried over. He must have been watching in the mirror, or maybe he had some kind of sixth sense, because Gwen heard the doors unlock as she approached.

She opened the passenger door and climbed in beside him. The door thudded solidly shut behind her, sealing them in, and Gwen felt the sense of security, the reassuring protective embrace of the big vehicle, enhanced considerably by the presence of Jack in the next seat.

He smiled at her. 'A little late, aren't we? For the big stakeout? I mean, I've been here since dawn. What if I'd needed to go for a pee?'

Gwen settled into her seat. There was a pair of binoculars resting on the dashboard, and she picked them up. 'Sorry,' she said. 'Did you?'

'Did I what?'

'Need to go for a pee.' She opened the binoculars, widening the device like a pair of smoothly articulated wings, until the graceful eyepieces were spread to match the spacing of her eyes.

'No. Fortunately. Where were you?'

'Personal time.'

Jack chuckled. 'Doing what?'

'It's called personal time because it's personal, Jack.' She adjusted the focus on the binoculars until she could see a group of young men – teenage boys actually – in the regulation T-shirts and hoodies and trainers, though with fewer, reflected Gwen, than the expected number of baseball caps. Maybe she was getting behind the times. Out of step with youth fashion. She'd have to refresh her catalogue of stereotypes.

'All right, Cactus Woman,' said Jack. 'Don't tell me then.'

'Why Cactus Woman?'

'Prickly,' said Jack, shaking his hand as though stung. 'With all these *sharp needles* sticking out. You reach out to touch Cactus Woman, just to make some kind of friendly contact with her, and *ouch*.'

'All right. I get the idea. Well if you must know I had to visit the doctor.'

For a moment Jack's face registered intense interest and more than a little surprise. '*The Doctor*? Oh, not "the" Doctor. You mean *your* doctor. Your GP.'

'Yes. The practice nurse, actually.'

'Nothing serious, I hope.'

'Woman's stuff.'

'Oh now you've gone and gotten me interested.'

Gwen shrugged. 'It's nothing. Just the results of some tests.'

'And they were all right? The results of the tests?'

'It's nothing. Everything's fine. It's just what they call sexual health.'

'Oh boy, now I'm really interested.'

'Grow up, Jack. I'm fine. Fine and fertile.'

Jack was silent for a moment, watching her closely, the trace of a smile on his face. 'So does this mean we can soon expect a little Gwen or a little Rhys scampering around the Hub?'

'Obviously not,' snapped Gwen.

'Why obviously?'

'Well, for a start, can you imagine anyone who would actually let a child run around loose in a place like that?' She remembered her own first impression of the Hub as, among many other things, a chamber of horrors.

'Their Uncle Jack might. He would let them see where their

Mummy worked. And then their Uncle Jack would let them scamper around the office a bit. Under careful supervision of course.'

'No their Uncle Jack bloody wouldn't. And anyway there aren't going to be any children scampering around.'

'It's all just hypothetical,' said Jack, nodding helpfully.

'Not even hypothetical. Nothing's going to happen. I'm not going to get pregnant. Not any time soon. Not while I'm working here.'

'Here?'

'Torchwood, I mean. This job is all too difficult and complicated and... dangerous.' She picked up the binoculars.

Jack sighed. 'Pity. I quite fancied being Uncle Jack for a minute there.'

'You're not my brother,' said Gwen. 'You couldn't be an uncle to my kids.' Then, relenting a little, 'Maybe a godfather.' She peered through the binoculars, adjusting the focus, her eyes probing at the slum supermarket across the road. Her roving gaze returned once again to the group of young men hanging around outside the main entrance.

In the seat beside her, Jack leaned back and sighed again. 'Godfather, eh? OK, thanks, I guess. But as a famous writer once said, "always a godfather and never a god".'

'Who was that? Arthur Machen?'

'No,' said Jack. 'Now since you're hogging the binoculars, why don't I fill you in on all the things that have been happening here in this cheerful inner-city neighbourhood? OK. Just before first light, a bunch of young men emerged from the Machen wearing the sort of rucksacks that teenagers normally carry on their way to school. These are the same kids you're looking at over there that we're talking about.'

'But these lads don't go to school,' said Gwen. She lowered the binoculars and looked at him.

'Right. That's right. Instead they go over to that double-decker bus.' He pointed through the smoked glass of the windshield. Gwen lifted the binoculars and looked.

The supermarket was surrounded by a car park of pitted concrete. Across the car park, abandoned and upended trolleys lay on their sides like dead buffalo with jutting legs, creating an obstacle course for the few battered cars that nosed in and out of the lot in a desultory fashion, exhausts throbbing.

And sure enough Gwen saw that among the parked vehicles there was a custard-yellow double-decker bus sitting, apparently permanently parked, beside the recycling bins that backed into the shadows behind the Happy Price. The bus said 'City Tours' on its side, but it didn't look to Gwen as if it had toured any cities in a long, long time.

'So these lads walk across the road and across the car park, heading over there to that bus. They apparently have a bit of trouble getting the bus doors open, and when they finally do, a sleepy-looking kid emerges. Obviously he's been asleep on the bus and gets what from this distance looks like a proper old-fashioned chewing-out from that kid there – Nobody Knows I'm a Lesbian.'

The figure in question was wearing a T-shirt, and the slogan Jack had just quoted was printed in bold white letters on its black cotton. However, it was clear that the T-shirt-wearer in question was not a lesbian of any description but in fact a hulking young man with dagger-shaped black sideburns jutting from below his black baseball cap and a sharply razored goatee beard. The knees that emerged from his baggy black shorts were stubby, hairy, heavily muscled and powerful. The kid wore black athletic socks on his bulging calves and all-black trainers. He was evidently the leader of the small group.

Jack turned and looked at her. 'And why do you think he was so angry at this kid? The kid from the bus, Sleepy?'

'Well,' said Gwen, 'because Sleepy was supposed to be the sentry on the bus. And he was asleep on the job.'

'Right,' said Jack. 'That's what I figured. The kid was guarding the bus. Which makes sense because they then give the kid all these rucksacks they're all wearing. Sleepy takes them and puts them on the bus.'

'And then Sleepy gets back in the bus and stays watching them,' said Gwen. 'Watching these bags.'

'Right,' said Jack. 'And hopefully he's not too sleepy this time. I don't reckon he will be, not after the nerve jangling chewing-out he got from Nobody Knows.'

'So they're bringing drugs out of the Machen in their rucksacks, and stowing them on the bus. To be accessed as and when they need them throughout the day.'

'That's right,' said Jack, grinning. 'You know, you'd make a very good police officer. Has anybody ever told you that? Or maybe a very good drug dealer. You have a devious criminal mind.'

'Thank you.'

'Anything else you've gleaned with that devious criminal mind?'

'Well you wouldn't sell directly out of the bus, now, would you?'

'No, you're right, Nobody Knows I'm a Lesbian and his gang actually do business in the open, in front of the supermarket, right there where you see them now.'

'Right there in the open?'

'Yup.'

'And that's where the drugs change hands?'

'No, they don't change hands there, that's the clever bit.' Jack smiled at her and Gwen silently cursed herself for not seeing it right away.

She said, 'They take the money from customers. Then they send them somewhere else to pick up the drugs.'

'Correct.'

'Which are stashed.'

'Correct. It's kind of self-serve. After they pay, they're told where to pick up their purchase. And they don't have far to go to get it. Just to those kiddie rides over there. You know, the kind you put a coin in and the kids get a shaky kind of ride? In the old days it was rocking horses. I remember those.'

Jack's voice was wistful for a moment, his eyes focused on other, inner scenes.

'You'd be surprised what you can get up to on a rocking horse. Assuming it's a sufficiently sturdy model. Anyway, nowadays it's all kinds of fancy rides.'

An unsettling thought struck Gwen. 'What happens if

123

some little kiddie wants to go on one of those fancy rides? Where they're stashing the drugs?'

'Well, then they'll get more than they bargained for from their fifty pence.'

Gwen stared across at him. 'This isn't a joke, Jack.'

He just shrugged and smiled. 'If it's any comfort, I haven't seen any kids around, except for one baby being pushed in a pram, and it was way too young to want to use any of those exciting novelty rides.'

'It?' said Gwen sharply. 'He or she, Jack. Babies aren't *its*. And what happens when it grows up? When it's big enough to want to go on those rides. Surrounded by these dealers.'

'You said "it"!' said Jack, grinning slyly and wagging a finger at her. She was tempted to grab his waving finger and squeeze it painfully. There were times when Gwen found Jack's cocky attitude quite annoying.

Other times he almost scared her, and could send a ripple of chills chasing in sequence down her spine. On those occasions, it was not so much the way he behaved, but the things that he said.

And this was one of those occasions. What he now said was, 'And anyway, some babies are an "it". Not where you come from, maybe. But that's just because you're lucky.'

Gwen lifted the binoculars again and stared through the windshield. 'So what else did you learn during your lonely pre-dawn vigil?'

'That's about it. But now that you're here we can get started properly.'

'Doing what?'

Jack was already reaching for the door and Gwen found herself doing the same.

'Looking for an alien heat-weapon.'

They locked the SUV and crossed the road towards the Happy Price. As they did so, an old-fashioned Volkswagen Beetle slowed down and pulled into the supermarket car park. It was painted silver and had a sticker on the rear bumper that read 'I'd Rather Be Fishing'.

'How do we find the weapon?' asked Gwen.

Jack held up his hand and showed Gwen his wrist-strap.

'And that will detect the energy signature?'

'It will if we get close enough,' he told her.

As they entered the car park, the door of the Volkswagen sprung open and a burly middle-aged man climbed laboriously out. He was wearing a brown corduroy jacket with green elbow patches, old worn blue jeans sagging on a thin tan belt that looked like it had had some extra holes punched to accommodate a swelling pot belly, and Doc Martens. On his head he wore a battered narrow-brim straw hat with a wide black band. Stuck in the band for decoration was a fishing lure, a bright hook with a rainbow tuft of tail. Apparently, as the man's bumper sticker proclaimed, he'd rather be fishing. He certainly didn't look pleased to be there.

The man took a briefcase out of the car, locked the car door, then put his head down like a rugby forward charging, and hurried towards the front doors of the Happy Price. As he neared the entrance, Gwen could hear the jeering voices of the lads. The man ignored them and trotted briskly into the supermarket, disappearing through its automatic doors.

'You want to get close to that lot?' Gwen eyed Nobody Knows I'm a Lesbian and his gang, still laughing happily at the fishing man's ignominious flight past them into the sanctuary of the Happy Price. It was obvious that they'd intimidated him and were proud of it. But none of them seemed to be in possession of any kind of bag or carrier. Nothing to hide a gun in. She thought about what Jack had said: they'd been depositing their rucksacks on the bus. 'You think this weapon is small enough that one of them might be concealing it on his person?'

'The problem is,' said Jack, 'we don't know exactly what we're looking for. It could be anything from the size of a great big beefy bazooka right down to a dainty little derringer.'

'Something that small could do the sort of damage we saw?' Gwen remembered the segmented body of Rhett Seyers, lying on its two autopsy tables.

'You'd be amazed,' said Jack. 'There's all kinds of wicked technology out there. But if they are packing anything we'll find out soon enough.'

'I want to go on the record as saying I don't find that very reassuring.'

'Noted. Now, just walk casually past them.'

'Casually past them, on the way to where?' said Gwen.

'To that nice little photo booth there.' Jack pointed and Gwen saw that, just beyond the three children's rides, there was indeed a small booth with a curtained doorway that offered passport-sized photos for anyone with five pounds in coins to spare. 'We'll get our picture taken,' said Jack.

'*Our* picture?'

'Sure, we'll squeeze into the booth together and snuggle up as the flashbulbs pop, just like a couple of eager young lovers. It will be romantic.'

'It'll be romantic if no one has done a wee in there.'

Jack sighed. 'Always looking on the bright side. Are you Welsh by any chance? Hey fellas!' This last was directed at Nobody Knows I'm a Lesbian and his crew, who looked away in a pointed and surly fashion as Jack gave them a cheerful wave. He took Gwen's arm and they strolled past the lads like a couple out on a promenade to take the morning air – an incongruous notion in the rubbish-strewn car park of this ghetto supermarket.

The lads didn't look at them and maintained a hostile silence as they walked past. But they furtively kept a close eye on Gwen and Jack as they approached the kiddie rides. The nearest of these was a little purple elf who was pushing a kind of bicycle with a child-sized seat. Next to the elf was a polka-dot steam train with a smiling face, featuring long eyelashes and rouged lips to make it clear that this was a female tank engine and not the more famous and heavily copyright-protected one. Past that, pushing a wheelbarrow containing another kiddie seat, was a grinning builder with a bristling moustache.

As they drew abreast of the elf, Gwen saw Nobody Knows I'm a Lesbian's hand twitch towards the back of his black T-shirt, and she made a mental note that he probably had a gun there, tucked into the waistband of his shorts.

But Nobody Knows relaxed and moved his hand away again as Gwen and Jack passed the rides and continued on, heading for the photo booth. He turned away, and the other members of his crew also ignored them, taking their cue from their leader.

Jack and Gwen slowed their pace. Jack surreptitiously checked his wrist-strap. 'Nothing,' he said.

'Did you get close enough?'

'Definitely.'

'Not a sausage?'

Jack grinned at her. 'Not a sausage, no. None of them had the heat-weapon on their person, or stashed anywhere nearby.'

'So what do we do now?'

'Guess we use the photo booth. We've come all this way looking like we're going to get our picture taken; it might seem suspicious if we don't follow through.'

Gwen nodded. 'It might at that. Why else would anyone be in this godforsaken place?'

'Right, so get your godforsaken picture taken.'

'Me?' said Gwen. 'What about you?'

'Think I'll go for a stroll. Continue in this direction and mosey around the back of the Happy Price.'

'Why? What's there?'

'Absolutely nothing, as far as I know. But if I keep walking…'

'You'll come back out by the bus,' said Gwen. 'Approaching it from behind the supermarket, where no one is likely to see you.'

'My thinking exactly.'

'But they have someone on the bus keeping a lookout.'

Jack nodded. 'Our friend Sleepy. I'll try not to wake him up.'

'It could be dangerous, Jack. Let me come with you.'

Jack shook his head. 'I'll be fine. I don't actually need to get on the bus. Just close to it. Close enough for this to work.' He touched his wrist-strap. 'See you back at the car in five.' Then he was gone.

Gwen reluctantly drew the dusty dark blue curtain aside and stepped into the photo booth and sat gingerly on the pale blue rotating stool. She adjusted the height of her stool and peered at her reflection in the scarred rectangle of glass facing her, and followed the instructions printed below it. Fortunately her prediction about the booth having been used as a public lavatory had proved wrong.

In fact, astonishingly, despite the graffiti that marred every available surface, the machine functioned perfectly well and, after a punctual series of flashes, dispensed a perfectly adequate and actually quite flattering set of passport photos. They clattered into the slot in front of her, still wet from the developing bath, and she picked them up carefully by one corner.

Pity she didn't need a passport, she thought. The curtain suddenly swept back with a harsh ratcheting noise, throwing daylight on her face. Gwen reached for her sidearm, but before her fingers could touch the gun, she was relaxing again. It was Jack, standing silhouetted there.

'Let's see,' he said, reaching for the photos. She passed

them to him. He studied them, frowning, 'Couldn't you have managed a smile?'

'I thought we were going to meet back at the car.'

Jack shrugged and handed the photos back to her. 'That was when I thought I might have had something interesting to report.'

'No luck with the bus, then?'

'Nope.'

'So what do we do now?'

Jack stepped aside as she emerged from the booth. 'Well, first I suggest some good old-fashioned police work. Think you can remember how to do that?'

'I'll do my best,' said Gwen tartly.

'Right then, let's go ask some questions.' He took Gwen's arm and led her towards the Happy Price.

Nobody Knows I'm a Lesbian and his crew studiously ignored them as they walked past. The supermarket was a low rectangular building of tan brick with a large sign on it featuring the words 'Happy Price' and a crude cartoon of an excitable, possibly rabid, pound sterling sign leaping up and down, grinning and revealing rather alarmingly sharp teeth which seemed to Gwen to be bared in apparent readiness to rip the throat out of any unsuspecting shopper.

As they approached the automatic doors, the man they'd seen earlier, with the corduroy jacket and the hat with the fishing lure, emerged from inside. He looked even less happy than he had before and visibly braced himself to run the gauntlet of loitering young men.

Gwen spared a sympathetic backwards glance for him

as she followed Jack through the sliding doors and into the Happy Price.

Inside the supermarket they learned two things, and the first came as quite a shock to Gwen. While they walked along the aisles she studied the prices of the merchandise and was astounded at how dear everything was. 'You'd think in a neighbourhood like this it would be bargain prices, not cut-throat ones.'

Jack shrugged. 'I guess it's the only place around here for people to shop.' He grinned at her. 'Being poor is an expensive business.'

'Yeah. Funny how you forget after a while…'

The second thing they learned was a rather more useful piece of information and came from the manager of the Happy Price. He was a plump, freckled Englishman named Bailey who, as it turned out, might have been a greedy bugger but also knew a great deal about what was going on outside his doors. He followed the local situation closely and told them that poor bisected Rhett Seyers had been a member 'in good standing' of the gang hanging around outside the supermarket. The current rumour circulating had Rhett Seyers stepping dangerously out of line with his gang. He had reportedly been selling drugs on the side, and thus was marked for death. 'The word on the street' was that he had been executed by his own gang.

Gwen and Jack thanked the man and headed for the exit.

'So much for my theory,' said Jack.

'Which theory was that?'

'Rival gangs. Gang warfare.'

'What about the alien vigilante?' said Gwen.

'That's another theory that bites the dust if our manager friend back there is right.'

'But we don't know that he's right,' said Gwen. 'He's just passing on gossip and rumour.'

'Nothing wrong with a bit of gossip and rumour,' said Jack. 'But it still leaves us with the problem of locating a very nasty piece of alien weaponry. What next?'

'Have a wander around the estate?'

Jack looked at Gwen with approval. 'We'll do a little tour, stroll past the front door of every flat if necessary. And if the weapon is hidden inside any of them, this will tell us.' He grinned and patted his wrist-strap.

They walked through the automatic doors and back out into the daylight. Gwen was surprised to see that Nobody Knows and his gang were gone. Then she spotted them, on the other side of the car park, pursuing a young mother. They were jeering at her and shouting 'Pram Face! Pram Face!' The girl had her head down and was busy pushing the pram in question, trying to escape her tormentors.

Gwen stared at the spectacle and said. 'Jack, do you mind if I…'

His eyes were also on the gang and the girl, and when he turned to Gwen he must have read the expression on her face because he said, 'Sure, go ahead. Catch up with me when you're done.' He set off towards the Machen Estate, then looked back over his shoulder. 'Don't be too hard on them!' He grinned.

With this vote of confidence ringing in her ears, Gwen headed over towards the young mother. As she trotted across the car park, she repressed the urge to increase her pace to an all-out dash. That would be the wrong way to enter the situation. A low-key approach was called for. And indeed at first no one even noticed that she had joined the baying throng. But then Nobody Knows I'm a Lesbian happened to glance her way and fell silent.

The rest of his gang rapidly followed suit and suddenly everyone was staring at her. Everyone except the young mother, who stood clutching her pram, head down, staring at the ground. Gwen realised that she was just a girl, no more than a teenager – like the gang who circled her.

'Can I help you?' said Nobody Knows, in an absurd burlesque of politeness.

'Yes,' said Gwen. 'Leave her alone.'

Nobody Knows I'm a Lesbian grinned slowly. He looked at the young mother, then back at Gwen. 'Oh, I don't think so.'

'I'm afraid I'm going to have to insist.' Gwen stepped forward, moving towards the girl. One of the gang members moved to stop her, a thin pockmarked boy with cornrows dyed an incongruous blond. As he reached out for her, Gwen grabbed his arm and reversed it into a tight, efficient arm-lock. The boy grunted with pain and, as if this were a signal, Nobody Knows put a hand behind his back, reaching under his T-shirt. Gwen instantly let go of the boy and drew her sidearm.

She pointed it at Nobody Knows I'm a Lesbian. 'Drop it,' she said. 'Take it out very slowly and very carefully and just drop it on the ground.' For a moment it looked as if he was going to ignore her and do something else, but the unwavering dark muzzle of her gun must have made an impression on him. His hand emerged with great slowness and care from under his T-shirt and revealed a heavy chromed revolver that had been concealed in his waistband. Gwen watched him open his hand and drop it. She noticed he extended one of his black trainers so the gun hit the toe of the shoe and cushioned its landing. He obviously didn't want the chrome getting scratched.

'Now step back. All of you.' The young men moved away from her quickly, only Nobody Knows lingering for a moment, reluctant to leave his gun.

'Now piss off.' They stared at her in surprise, suddenly looking like a bunch of kids again, and then they turned away and started slinking off. Slinking quickly turned to running. As they dispersed, Gwen picked up the revolver, checking to make sure the hammer wasn't cocked, and put it away in a pocket of her jacket. She then holstered her own side arm and turned to the young mother, intending to say something. To offer some words of comfort.

But her eyes were drawn irresistibly to the baby in the pram. It was a radiant, beautiful baby. Chubby and chortling, bright-eyed and happy, blissfully unaware of the drama that had been taking place around it. He – it was presumably a boy, judging by his adorable powder-blue garb – was busy counting his fingers and drooling. Gwen, stared into the pram, hypnotised by this cute little chap in his spotless romper suit. Absurdly, she found broody feelings welling up in herself. She had to physically tear her eyes away from the baby and concentrate on the mother, by contrast a strangely drained and listless figure.

The girl had long, straight, hair which was a little too pale to be called mousy. Her washed-out blue eyes stared at Gwen without interest. At first glance, the girl looked painfully thin, but then Gwen noticed the supple bulge of muscles on the girl's bare arms and the etched lines of tendons which showed under that white skin. She wasn't skinny. She was lean and sinewy.

The girl reminded Gwen of some people she'd come across a few years ago, who'd run a yoga ashram, placid celibates with the same kind of colourless look, sort of healthy but unhealthy at the same time: washed out, pale skin, colourless hair as though deprived of something vital. At the time, Gwen had assumed it was sex.

'Are you all right?' she said.

'Yeah.' The girl nodded as if she'd just exchanged a passing everyday pleasantry with a nodding acquaintance and turned away, busily pushing her pram across the car park as if nothing had happened.

Gwen watched her for a moment, then hurried after her. 'Wait a minute,' she called, but the girl didn't slow down. Gwen had to run to catch up with her. The girl was setting an impressive pace, the pram wheels buzzing across the stained tarmac.

Falling into step beside her, Gwen said, 'Can we talk for a minute?'

'Got to get on.' The girl kept moving and didn't look at her.

With some effort, Gwen managed to keep pace with her as she walked, and she tried to draw the girl out, but the girl remained monosyllabic and unforthcoming. Gwen might also with some justice have added *ungrateful* and *surly* – but perhaps this would have been reading too much into that pasty, blank, hangdog face. It was a beaten-down face. A victim's face.

They crossed the road and reached the east gate of the Machen Estate, at which point Gwen simply gave up. The girl seemed determined to ignore her, to brush off any attempt at help. So be it. Gwen watched the girl go, pushing her pram into the shadows of the concrete jungle where she lived. Gwen watched with a mixture of frustration and regret. Just then she saw Jack emerge from the west gate down the street. He had seen her and was beckoning to her. He looked pleased with himself. They met on the pavement, halfway between the two gates. He had taken off his greatcoat and was using it to cover an object slightly smaller than a cricket bat.

'You've found it,' said Gwen.

'That's right. In a flat in Bowmen House. Ground floor. I went in and retrieved it.' He opened the coat to show her what, for all its strange alien contours and curvature and nacreous gleam, was obviously a gun of some kind.

'How did you get into the flat?'

'I used a highly sophisticated device I've perfected for breaking into locked domiciles.' Jack winked at her. 'I smashed a window with my elbow.'

'You take very naturally to vandalism, Jack Harkness.'

Jack grinned. 'Baby, I'm a vandal and a Visigoth too.'

'Speaking of babies, I just saw the most beautiful one.'

Jack glanced at her in surprise. There must have been a reminiscent tenderness in her tone of voice she couldn't quite conceal. 'Hey!' he said. 'You're smitten.'

'Honestly, Jack, he was so adorable.'

Jack shook his head. 'It pays for babies to be adorable. That's kind of a baby's business. It's their raison d'être, so to speak.'

'You're just an old cynic.'

'No, seriously. Nothing wrong with a baby being cute. It has high survival value.'

Gwen was about to repeat some variation on her accusation of cynicism, but there was the sound of running footsteps behind them and she turned quickly, her hand on her gun. She was half-expecting an onslaught of reprisal by the drugs gang. On reflection, they seemed to have been all too easily cowed.

But instead it was the man in the corduroy jacket and fishing hat. He had apparently been sitting in his car eating a sandwich. The door of his silver Volkswagen, still parked across the street, was open and the man himself was still clutching the half-eaten sandwich, a bright red shred of tomato dangling from it as he hurried towards them.

'Wait, please,' he called. 'I saw what happened—'

'What happened?' said Jack, stopping and carefully holding the wrapped weapon so there was no danger of the man seeing it.

'Your colleague here…' The man looked at Gwen.

'Who said she was my colleague?'

'I saw you together earlier.'

'Perhaps she's my sweetheart. Maybe we're not colleagues at all.'

'I think you are,' said the man obstinately. 'And what's more I think you're some kind of police unit.'

'No,' said Jack.

'Well maybe sort of,' said Gwen at the same moment.

'I knew it!' said the man. 'I've learned to recognise you – fellow professionals – doing the work I do.'

Jack shook his head dubiously. 'And what work is that?'

'Social worker. Here, my card. Kenrick Jones.' He handed them a business card. Jack glanced at it and pocketed it.

'Well,' he said, smiling one of his bright, charming smiles. 'Nice to meet you, Kenrick, now if you'll excuse us…'

'More specifically, I am the social worker assigned to Pam Feerce.'

'Who?' said Gwen.

'You met her. You helped her. She's the one those boys were bothering, before you helped her.'

'Pam Feerce?'

'Yes. That's what she's called. Hence the nickname, I suppose. Pram Face.'

As they stood there on the pavement in front of the Machen Estate, Jack obviously itching to be gone, Kenrick Jones insisted on telling them about the girl's case. It was a troubling one. She had been a friendless teenager, so fat that nobody even noticed she was pregnant. Gwen found it hard

138

to reconcile this description with the tautly drawn, sinewy figure she had just encountered. But the other details of the social worker's story accorded with the drab, blank-faced girl. Deeply introverted, her only passion, indeed her only interest in life had been the school chess club.

'Second only to the science club in winning friends,' said Jack.

Kenrick Jones frowned. 'No, being in the chess club is actually very unpopular among coevals.'

'Yes, we get that,' said Gwen evenly.

The social worker nodded and went on, describing how the baby had become the sole focus of Pam Feerce's life. Spending all day caring for the child, she had isolated herself completely. Her few friends (more like acquaintances, really) from the chess club had been unceremoniously dropped. She had equally little trouble cutting herself off from the surviving members of her (highly dysfunctional) family. And she had also cut herself off from society at large.

'She has never even registered her baby's birth. She and the child have no official existence. They are in danger of slipping through the system entirely.'

'OK,' said Jack with forced patience. 'Fascinating. Both sad and fascinating. But why are you telling us all this?'

'Because I want your help.'

'Our help?'

'I saw your colleague face down the Dillard gang,' said Kenrick. 'You can help me. I know you can.' He paused and looked at the ornate brick façade of the Machen Estate. 'This is a no-go area for social workers. The police can't help me.'

He looked at them. 'The ordinary police, I mean. They don't have the resources. If anybody can help, it's you.' He tried a tentative smile.

Gwen was tempted to say yes. But Jack had other ideas. 'We're not social workers.'

Kenrick Jones tightened his shoulders and lowered his head in the same manner Gwen had seen when he was preparing to run the gauntlet of the gang. He shook his head stubbornly. 'Like it or not, she's your responsibility.'

'How do you figure that?' Jack's voice had taken on an edge and Gwen could see the situation going downhill rapidly. He was giving Kenrick Jones a hard look now, staring straight into his eyes.

But the social worker stared back levelly and said, 'When your friend intervened with the gang, they lost status. They lost face.' He glanced at Gwen. 'She humiliated them. And now they'll be out for revenge.'

Jack grinned, but his eyes were hard. 'They're not going to harm one hair on Gwen's head.'

Gwen was annoyed at Jack's obtuseness in the matter but she didn't have to say anything to set him straight. The social worker was already busy explaining it for her.

'Of course not,' he said. 'I meant they'll go after Pam Feerce. She's a marked woman now.'

'Right,' said Ianto. He steepled his fingers and frowned thoughtfully. 'Let's decide who has confiscated the most interesting weapon.'

On a rectangle of smooth black cloth spread across a

workbench in front of him were two very dissimilar guns: the gleaming chrome revolver Gwen had taken from Nobody Knows I'm a Lesbian, and the alien heat-weapon Jack had found in the Machen Estate. Gwen watched with a crooked smile. She knew what was coming. Jack was sitting there, also smiling. He knew too.

'Well, I'm afraid,' said Ianto finally, 'that it has to be Jack. Very good attempt though, Gwen, with this highly polished example of drug-dealer bling.' He prodded the revolver with a pencil as though it was a distasteful specimen of some small dead pest.

'It's a Colt Python .357 with a four-inch barrel, actually,' said Gwen. 'A fairly dangerous weapon.'

'Good try, Gwen.' Ianto paused to sip his coffee. 'But I'm afraid however long its barrel is—'

'That's a short barrel, as a matter of fact.'

'Or however short it is,' continued Ianto, unperturbed, 'it just doesn't hold a candle to this.' He tapped the alien heat-gun with his pencil. The pencil was reflected, a soft polychrome shape, in the smooth rainbowed curves of the weapon. Ianto tossed the pencil aside and lifted a corner of the black cloth. He folded it so that the revolver was covered, leaving only the pearly shape of the heat-gun on display. 'In the end, there's no contest, really.' He took a sip of his coffee. 'Jack confiscated the best gun by far today.'

'Well, thank you, Ianto,' said Jack, putting his hand to his chest and offering a slight bow.

Ianto set his cup aside. 'Just one thing, Jack.'

Jack's eyebrows angled upwards in polite enquiry. 'Yeah?'

'I checked this heat-weapon against our catalogue of alien guns…'

'We still have one of those?'

'On our database, yes.'

'How cool is that?'

'Yes, but unfortunately, Jack, as a result of checking this database and learning a bit more about this weapon, its specifications and so on, I've uncovered a disturbing fact.'

'How disturbing?'

'I've discovered that it has never been fired.'

Both Gwen and Jack were staring at him now. Gwen felt a cold feeling starting deep in her stomach.

'What?' said Jack.

'This particular weapon,' said Ianto patiently, 'has never been fired. The factory seal is still intact, so to speak.'

'So it's not the gun we were looking for,' said Gwen.

'No, that one would still be at large.'

'Back to square one,' said Gwen with a note of bitterness in her voice.

'It's a goldmine of information,' said Jack, who sounded much the same, 'this database of yours.' He looked at Ianto.

'It certainly is,' said Ianto.

The cold feeling of dread in Gwen's stomach had time enough now to have turned to anger. 'In fact, there could be any number of these guns out there.'

'I think just one more,' said Ianto.

'How can you be sure?'

'Well I'm not sure, but it's an educated guess, based on the aforementioned goldmine of information. You see, the database also told me that this gun normally comes in a twin configuration.'

'What do you mean?' said Gwen. 'Do you mean like a double-barrelled shotgun?'

Ianto nodded. 'Yes, if you can imagine a shotgun that instead of merely having two barrels was actually two complete weapons, linked together.'

'Siamese twins,' said Jack.

'Exactly. You could use such guns as a double unit or separate them whenever you wanted.' He touched a kind of circular socket on the side of the gun. 'There. You see that indentation there? That's where it locks onto its twin. Each part can be used individually as a weapon in its own right but it's also rather cleverly designed to join up in the paired unit which, rather alarmingly, would provide twice the firepower.'

Gwen closed her eyes and tried to imagine what twice the firepower of this thing would imply. Two versions of Rhett Seyers cut into a total of four pieces. And no doubt things much worse.

'So to sum up, yes, Gwen you're right. It's exactly like a double-barrelled shotgun, except a thousand times more powerful and dangerous.' Ianto looked at her, smiling.

'No need to be pedantic,' said Gwen.

'The point is,' said Jack, 'we don't want it to fall into the wrong hands.'

'Hard to imagine what the right hands would be.'

'Well, they'd have four fingers and an opposable thumb for a start.'

'You think this gun would be safer if a human being got hold of it?'

Jack nodded. 'As opposed to an alien who understands its full capabilities and knows exactly how to exploit them? Sure.'

Gwen regarded him sardonically. 'Unlike an ignorant human being who might accidentally press the wrong button and blow the whole thing up, along with a substantial portion of Cardiff.'

'Actually, it's funny you should say that,' said Ianto, 'because it does in fact have a self-destruct facility. Not exactly a button, more a—'

'OK, OK,' said Jack. 'You've convinced me. The only safe hands are Torchwood hands. So let's get out there and find the damned thing.'

The afternoon sun was shining down on the Machen Estate as they pulled up outside. Gwen was secretly quite glad to be back there. Ever since they'd left the place that morning she had been worrying about what might have happened to Pam Feerce. The social worker's words were still echoing in her ears.

She tried again to convince Jack, but he just shook his head and said, 'You can't take responsibility for that girl.'

'Jack, I also can't let her come to harm.'

'Fine. So what are you going to do? Mount a guard on her twenty-four hours a day?'

'Obviously not. No, I thought I'd have a word with Nobody Knows I'm a Lesbian. Put the fear of God into him.'

Jack smiled. 'Well, there our interests coincide. That heat-weapon may not have been exactly the one we were after, but I'd still be very interested to find out where that joker and his gang got it. Once we do that we'll be a lot closer to finding its twin.'

They got out of the SUV and immediately heard the shouting. It was coming from the direction of the supermarket. There were shouts of rage and abuse and high-pitched shrieks of pain.

There in the car park in front of the Happy Price, a milling mass of bodies was moving in a violent parody of a folk dance, surging abruptly in one direction and then another, following the abruptly shifting focus of the violence.

Gwen instantly broke into a run. Jack was already in motion, at her side. They pelted across the road, towards the car park, where Nobody Knows I'm a Lesbian and his gang were attacking Pam Feerce. Although, as they grew nearer, they realised it would be more accurate to say that Pam Feerce was attacking the gang.

As Gwen approached the heaving mass of bodies, a figure was thrown through the air towards her, slamming to the ground to lie painfully still at her feet. She recognised the youth with the blond cornrows whom she had placed in an arm-lock earlier. He was in even worse shape now, beginning to writhe on the dirty car park tarmac, gasping for air and clutching his side. As she ran past him – no time to stop now – she fleetingly diagnosed broken ribs, judging by the angle of the foot she had seen flash out of the crowd as it kicked him across the car park.

A foot that belonged to Pam Feerce.

The girl wasn't just kicking, though. She was also punching, with considerable effect. Gwen arrived just in time to see her drive her left fist into the belly of one of the gang members and, a fraction of a second later, her right fist into the throat of one of the others in what looked like a brutal, and potentially fatal, blow. As she threw the second punch, her left elbow came up into the face of a third attacker.

All three of them went down, writhing.

'OK, that's enough!' shouted Jack, pulling out his gun.

There were six of the gang left on their feet at this moment, confronting a pale, sweating, but very focused and determined-looking Pam Feerce. Three of the gang members ignored Jack, or perhaps didn't hear him. They were already in the act of throwing themselves on the girl. Three other members of the gang hesitated, standing back from the fighting. Of these three, one was a boy Gwen didn't recognise, the second was Sleepy, the boy who had been guarding the bus, and the third was Nobody Knows I'm a Lesbian.

At Jack's command the first two instantly raised their hands in surrender. But Nobody Knows turned and ran. 'Shall I go after him?' asked Gwen.

'No, let him go.' Jack held his gun on the other two for a moment, then decided they were no threat and turned to deal with the seething mêlée that was Pam Feerce and the three boys.

One boy had grabbed her left arm, another her right. The third threw himself down to grab her legs. He received a swift and well-aimed kick in the face for his trouble but bounced back up gamely and threw himself once again at the girl, who was now being held securely by the other two lads, unable to land a blow with both her arms pinned.

Jack moved in to intervene and Gwen started to do the same, but then she noticed the direction in which Nobody Knows was running. Towards the doors of the supermarket where, parked among a battered assortment of shopping trolleys, was the pram containing Pam Feerce's baby.

Nobody Knows was heading straight towards the pram and he had a gun in his hand. Gwen observed that it was an exact replica of the one she'd confiscated earlier. She turned and ran after him. Gwen couldn't quite believe what she was thinking – surely no one would dream of hurting an innocent baby?

But apparently, on some level, she could all too easily believe this, judging by the breathless speed with which she ran, and the force with which she tackled Nobody Knows, jumping on him from behind, slamming him to the ground. Before he could catch his breath, she was handcuffing him with the plastic 'zap straps' she carried. She sealed the straps around his wrists with painful tightness. She could see track-mark scars on his arms and realised he was at best an ex-user of much worse merchandise than the stuff he'd been selling.

She stood up, panting, as Nobody Knows cursed her in a ceaseless stream of inventive profanity. Gwen looked around and saw the chromed Colt revolver lying on the ground and, with a certain sense of déjà vu, picked it up, checked the hammer, and pocketed it. She turned back to look at the fracas. It seemed Jack had things under control, although he was sensibly making no effort to intervene between Pam Feerce and her three assailants. Instead he and the other, now surrendered, gang members were just watching the trio being savagely beaten by the girl.

Behind Gwen, Nobody Knows I'm a Lesbian was still swearing. She did her best to ignore the sound. And as she did so, what she heard instead was an oddly soft, sonorous voice saying, 'Thank you.'

She turned and looked around, but there was no one nearby. Inside the supermarket there was a clump of onlookers, avid, frightened faces pressed to the windows. But they were staying well out of it. And behind her was Jack and the gang members and the fight. And at her feet was the handcuffed Nobody Knows.

But there was no one else nearby. No one except...

Gwen went over to the pram and stared down at the baby lying there. He smiled, drool running down his chin, and stared up at her with his bright blue eyes and said, 'Thank you, Gwen.'

'No, really, thank you,' said the baby. 'He was running over here planning to put a bullet in me. Or at least, to threaten to do so. In any case, he intended to pull me out from under my nice warm blanket and wave me around in his big smelly hand while he pressed that nasty cold gun to my head. Altogether, an unpleasant prospect.'

The baby wasn't moving his mouth as he spoke. Instead, his words seemed to form spontaneously in Gwen's mind, like soap bubbles swelling and bursting and vanishing in a softly echoing space just behind her eyes. She rubbed her head and stared at him.

'But you saved me from all that,' said the baby.

'You're talking to me,' said Gwen, speaking out loud. 'Inside my head.'

'Yes.'

'How?'

The baby said, 'Well it helps that you are receptive, and also that I'm not human.'

'Not human?'

'No indeed. I came here through what you call the Rift. Was brought here, rather. By my... mother.' There was a tremulous hesitation on this word that caused Gwen's own tear ducts to fill. It was as if the baby's feelings were pouring into her mind along with his words.

Her own voice trembled with emotion as she spoke. 'She brought you here – and left you?'

'Yes. To use an image from your own memory, I was like the baby you once saw, found by your police colleagues, a baby who had been left abandoned in a carrier bag.'

Gwen was jolted by the mention of the incident. It had taken place five years earlier and had caused quite a stir at the time. The baby had been found abandoned in a churchyard. Luckily it had survived several hours of exposure and had later been successfully fostered. She remembered how there had been a pathetic bundle of five pound notes in the bag with the baby, like a bribe to the gods by some poor desperate mother asking whoever found the bag to take care of her child.

'Yes, exactly,' said the baby. 'That's why I chose that particular memory, for its aptness. Because I, too, was left with something. When my mother abandoned me and returned through the Rift to our homeworld, she left behind a "bribe", as you call it. Though it was not money. Something far more useful.'

'The gun?'

'That's right, a Torrosett 51 binary heat-cannon. And since you're wondering, I instructed Pam to take only one of the guns and leave the other one behind. After all, who needs more than one of those things?'

Gwen shook her head, trying to absorb this information, or perhaps trying to shake this strange voice out of it. 'You're an alien,' she said.

'Yes, the name of my race would be meaningless to you, as indeed would be my own name. But, associating thoughts and sounds that have similar emotional weightings for you, you could call me Czisch.'

'Czisch?' repeated Gwen.

'Yes, and you are Gwen, but I will call you Mummy!'

'Mummy?'

'Yes, I like you better than the other one. You are for me what I believe your people would term an *upgrade*. Yes, I will let go of the other one and take you. I think you are a splendid choice for Czisch. And right now Czisch needs comfort!' The voice became suddenly shrill and troubled. 'Needs picking up! Bad man nearly hurt me! Pick me up!'

Gwen moved without thought or hesitation to the pram and scooped up the small, warm, living bundle. She held the baby to her face and breathed its intoxicating smell. 'There, there,' she said. 'Don't cry, poor baby. Everything's all right.'

Pam Feerce had finished very thoroughly beating up the three dealers and now stood panting over their recumbent forms.

Jack was just trying to work out the best way of tackling her himself when all at once the girl wavered on her feet and collapsed. He couldn't believe his luck. In fact, at first he suspected a trap. But she lay convincingly unmoving for some seconds, so he checked the handcuffs on his prisoners and left them where they were sitting, then moved forward to inspect her.

Pam stirred as he put a hand to her face and opened her eyes.

'It let go of me,' she said. And then her eyes filled with tears and she began to sob. She reached up for Jack, and before he could stop her she had wrapped her arms tightly around him, clinging and weeping. Pam Feerce seemed to have changed from an unstoppable fighting machine into a wilting flower, and it was a transformation which he didn't understand, though he wholeheartedly endorsed it.

As her tears soaked the lapel of his greatcoat, he looked around, a trifle embarrassed, to see what Gwen was up to. She was standing by the pram and holding the baby. Jack grinned. Typical.

But he relaxed now, and let the girl go on crying on his chest.

Everything was under control.

At least, that was what he thought until the girl stopped crying and said, 'Thank God. It's let go of me at last. I couldn't stand it. Like being a prisoner in my head.'

She stared up into Jack's face, imploring him to understand. He nodded as if he did, while he tried to piece together what she was saying.

'I'm never going back. Never going back.'

'That's all right,' he said. Automatic soothing words, while his mind raced. 'You won't have to.'

'I couldn't. I won't. I won't let it get me again. I'll kill myself. I would have killed myself before if I could. But it wouldn't let me. I was its slave. It made me do things. It was controlling me.'

Jack felt a chill as he began to realise what she was talking about.

'It even controlled me while it was asleep. Like a big iron fist holding my mind. I would have done anything to get away from it.'

Jack stared at her.

'I found it,' she said. 'I heard it crying in the bushes behind the Red Hand. I was coming home from school. Someone had just left it there. I couldn't believe it. I picked it up. That was the moment. I kept going back to that moment in my mind. Trying to change what happened. But I couldn't change anything. It was too late. I picked it up. And then it had me.'

She looked over Jack's shoulder at Gwen.

'And now it's got your friend.'

***

Jack activated his earpiece and called the Hub, keeping his eyes on Gwen and the baby. She was holding the baby in one arm, with the expert air of someone who was long experienced in so doing. With her other arm she had reached into the blankets in the pram and was probing them, looking for something. There was something strange about the way she moved, about her body language. With a small feeling of sickness, Jack realised it didn't look like Gwen at all.

'I got free of it!' said Pam Feerce, her voice began to quaver with renewed tears. 'And I'm never going back. Never going back.'

He ignored the girl as he heard Ianto come onto the line.

'Ianto,' he said, 'get over here.'

'What's up?'

Jack glanced at Pam Feerce, now kneeling sobbing on the ground. 'We worked out who was killing the drug dealers. Though it looks like self-defence instead of vigilantes or rival gangs.'

'And did you find the gun?' said Ianto.

'Yes.'

'Where was it?'

'In a baby's pram.'

'Well that was original, anyway,' said Ianto. 'You detected it with your wrist-strap?'

'No,' said Jack. 'I'm looking at it now.'

By the supermarket, Gwen had drawn the heat-gun out from under the blankets in the pram. It was an exact replica of the one back at the Hub. As Jack watched, she activated the gun so that it came to life and a searing red column of light poured out from its muzzle. Then, still holding the baby in one arm, she nonchalantly aimed it at the double-decker bus.

The red beam hit the yellow metal of the bus's roof with a searing noise like spit on a griddle. It caused a long line across the bus's roof to blister black, then turn molten red, then split open in a blaze of white sparks.

'You see,' sobbed Pam. 'She knows how to use it. He's showed her, just like he showed me. He made me take it home with him and he taught me how to use it, taught me all about it, all in a flash in my head.'

The double-decker fell noisily apart, sheared open at an awkward angle, like a giant slice of cake being cut. 'Get over here as quick as you can,' said Jack to Ianto.

'You have no idea what it was like,' moaned Pam tearfully, kneeling on the ground at Jack's feet. 'My life was gone. It stole my entire life.'

'Right,' said Ianto in Jack's ear.

'But before you leave,' said Jack, 'there's one thing I need you to do.'

'Nice, nice, nice,' cooed the baby in her mind.

'There,' said Gwen. 'Everything's all right.'

'Czisch needs feeding!' shrilled the baby. 'Hungry hungry hungry. Milk milk milk.'

'We'll go into the supermarket and get you something.'

'Yes, get me something!'

Gwen settled the baby back into the pram beside the heat-gun, carefully smoothing his blanket over him, and pushed the pram towards the supermarket. Inside she saw people scatter at her approach. She ignored them. She only had eyes for him, her gurgling baby boy.

The automatic doors whispered apart as she wheeled the pram inside.

Instead of taking a shopping cart, she used the pram itself, loading items into it, careful not to disturb the little person lying inside. She selected nappies and baby wipes and food, a great deal of baby food of every description. A distant part of her mind registered how absurdly high the price of everything was in here. But she ignored that; obviously it was not important. The important thing was getting lots of food and feeding her baby.

'Food food food,' said the cooing voice in her head. 'Eat eat eat.'

'Soon baby, soon,' crooned Gwen. She pushed the pram down the aisle, away from baby food, towards the checkouts. As she did so the doors of the supermarket opened and someone came in. Two people. Two figures that she recognised. Or thought she *should* recognise.

They were two men. One wore a military greatcoat. The other was smartly dressed in a business suit. They looked familiar. The one in the business suit handed the one in the greatcoat a sheet of paper. He accepted it and began to fold it.

They were looking at Gwen.

She realised that in some distant part of her mind she knew their names. But she didn't bother trying to remember. It wasn't important. They weren't important.

But their importance suddenly swelled when the one folding the paper stopped folding it and threw it into the air. It was a paper plane, although Gwen couldn't have given a name to the object as it sailed through the air. All her attention, her entire mind it seemed, was given over to watching the paper plane, following and anticipating its trajectory. It was coming towards the baby. Her baby. An object falling through the air. At her baby. Nothing must come near her baby. Not unless she knew it was safe.

She had no trouble snatching the paper plane out of the air before it landed. Her reflexes were lightning fast. Her every sense was keyed fine and sharp. She stared at the paper, crumpled in her hand. It had a photograph printed on it.

A man's face.

Even crumpled as it was, the face was recognisable.

'I'm hungry!' shrilled the baby's voice in her mind. But, for the first time, Gwen found herself able to ignore it. She smoothed the paper in her hands. The face from the photograph smiled up at her.

'Hungry hungry hungry!' came the voice in her head, redoubled in volume and intensity. It drove out the name that was forming in her mind, in response to the picture she held in her hand. But the face kept staring at her. And the name came inexorably back.

'Rhys.'

The baby started wailing stridently in her head. But Gwen ignored it and kept focusing on the photo and the name. She had a strange certainty that they were important. Vitally important.

And, as she concentrated, the baby's voice grew fainter and the face and name became more familiar. Memory started to come back, flowing like blood into a numb limb.

And with that flow came identity, and consciousness and control. Gwen turned away from the pram, where the baby was still screaming. But now it was wailing aloud, and it was the wordless cry of all infants who have yet to acquire language.

The two young men were grinning at her as she approached. Grinning in triumph. Their names came back to her. Jack first. And then Ianto. Through the glass door of the supermarket she could see into the car park. Out there a girl was kneeling on the ground. Gwen knew she should know that young woman's name too. But it was too soon. It was too hard for her to remember.

Or to recognise the significance of what was happening as the girl abruptly stiffened and rose from her knees, like a puppet suddenly being jerked up on invisible strings, being pulled by the controlling hand of its giant puppeteer.

Behind Gwen, the baby had stopped crying, as though it had found something to comfort it.

'Welcome back,' said Jack, grinning at her. 'Nice photo, huh?'

'Good job it did the trick,' said Ianto.

'I guess it really is true love.' Jack winked at her. 'We figured if anything would bring you back to yourself it would be Rhys. Good old Rhys.'

'How did you know what had happened to me?' said Gwen.

'Pam Feerce. She told me everything.' Jack suddenly stopped talking and all at once all three of them realised the same thing.

Pam was no longer in the car park outside. She had walked in through the automatic doors, down the baby food aisle, and was picking up the baby from its pram.

'Oh shit,' said Gwen.

'That's not good,' said Ianto.

Even from where she was standing, Gwen could see that something was very wrong with Pam Feerce. The girl seemed to be trembling uncontrollably. As she clutched the baby in one arm, she was delving under its blankets with the other.

Jack was the first to realise what she was doing, and he started shouting for everybody to get out of the supermarket. After what they'd already seen, it didn't take much to convince the staff and the few remaining shoppers to evacuate the premises. As they were hurried outside under Ianto's supervision, Jack and Gwen remained behind for a moment.

Pam had pulled the heat-gun out from the pram and was holding it in one hand while the other clutched the baby. It was a stance identical to Gwen's earlier. Except instead of firing the gun, Pam was staring at it, as if trying to remember something.

'Pam,' called Jack.

'Go away,' said the girl. Her voice was flat and forlorn.

'We can help you,' said Gwen.

'No you can't. Nobody can. It's got me again. In a minute I won't even be able to think my own thoughts.' The girl looked at them, her face pale and desperate. 'Get out! Now! I know what I've got to do.'

'What does she mean?' said Gwen. Her mind was still recovering from the alien grip which had recently held it so painfully tight, and it was functioning with maddening slowness.

But Jack seemed to understand. He was already dragging her out, through the automatic doors, into the car park.

'Everybody get back!' he yelled. 'As far away as you can!'

He helped Gwen and Ianto disperse the crowd, and they were all moving across the street towards the Machen Estate when the explosion came, on a shockwave of hot air and flying fragments of glass. The roof of the Happy Price rose up into the air like the wing of a big black bird, an orange globe of flame rising slowly under it. There was a sound like a thunderclap that made Gwen's ears ache.

But the noise and the conflagration seemed to clear her head. She knew what had happened. She looked at Ianto. 'The self-destruct button,' she said.

'It wasn't exactly a button,' said Ianto.

'Pam knew how to use the weapon, just like I did. The baby taught her about all its functions. But why…?'

Jack shrugged. 'I suppose she'd had a taste of freedom and she wasn't going back to being a slave.'

'She'd rather be dead?' said Gwen wonderingly. Then she remembered that iron grip on her mind. The feeling that no thought was her own, or ever would be again. To exist as a puppet always dancing to someone else's needs and whims. A life lived in servitude. She'd experienced it for a few minutes. She thought about what it must have been like to suffer that night and day, month after month.

She shuddered.

There was the distant sound of sirens as the black smoke poured up into the sky.

Virus

JAMES MORAN

'I can see the headlines now,' said Ianto. 'They'll have a field day. "Torchwood kills babies".'

'Hey – we didn't kill a baby,' said Jack. 'It wasn't a baby, it was an alien.'

'Yes,' said Ianto. 'An alien baby.'

The team walked into the Hub, covered in dust and dirt.

'Fine, an alien baby. But we didn't kill it. She activated the self-destruct, there was nothing we could do.'

'Just as well we left before the TV cameras arrived,' said Ianto. 'But someone's bound to have noticed us.'

'They won't even know we were there,' said Gwen. 'It was all fairly low-key. More or less. Apart from the supermarket blowing up. How are we going to explain that one, by the way?'

'Gas leak,' said Jack. 'I mentioned it to a deliciously firm-looking firefighter. Told him somebody complained about smelling gas a few hours before it happened. We can seed the story in the usual places, it won't be a problem.'

'Was that the one I saw you chatting to by the phone box?'

asked Gwen. 'Ooh, he was bloody lovely, he was. When he started unravelling that hose, I thought I was going to faint.'

'Some firefighting skills transfer very nicely to other areas,' said Jack, grinning.

'Hey,' said Gwen. 'I saw him first.'

'And you're taken,' said Ianto. 'Both of you are. Nothing wrong with window shopping, just try not to lick the glass so much.'

They walked down to the Boardroom and sat down. Ianto opened up three pizza boxes, and passed round bottles of beer. He presented the pizzas with a flourish.

'Fine dining, Torchwood style,' he said. 'There's no dessert, so make the most of it.'

Gwen smiled at him. 'It's perfect, thank you.'

She and Jack lifted their beer bottles as a salute to Ianto, who bowed appreciatively. 'I do my best,' he said. 'Which is usually pretty damn good, if I say so myself. Which I do.'

They ate the pizzas in silence, too tired to talk. Gwen would have preferred to be having dinner with Rhys, but he was out tonight with Banana Boat and Daf. She didn't want to be at home, eating by herself. She was glad of the company. Just another evening at Torchwood, sitting around together, with a takeaway.

Jack noticed a blinking light on the telephone screen. He raised his eyebrows. 'Twenty-seven messages. All from the same number. Detective Kathy Swanson. That can't be good.'

'Don't listen to them,' said Gwen. 'We already know what she's going to say.'

'True,' said Ianto. 'Blah blah blah, Torchwood are rubbish, you think you own the place, blah blah blah.'

'I know,' said Jack. 'But she might need help with something. And let's face it, we probably deserve a verbal kicking.'

The other two looked at him. He shrugged, and hit the redial button.

The police station looked like a paper bomb had hit it, and officers were frantically scrambling around trying to deal with the constant phone calls and reports. In the midst of it all, Detective Swanson was swearing spectacularly, employing some new and unusual combinations of words. A uniformed officer approached, and waited for a break in the swearing.

'What is it, Amy?'

The officer coughed. 'Phone call for you, ma'am.'

'Tell them I'm busy. We've got so many officers out on this bloody supermarket thing, we're having to prioritise and let some things go. Petty thieves are having a field day. Whatever it is, it'll have to wait.'

'Er, it's Torchwood.'

Swanson's head whipped around, and her eyes gleamed. 'Oh, really? Put them through to my desk.'

The officer nodded, and hurried off, glad that she wasn't involved in whatever was about to happen.

Jack waited on the line, holding the handset to his ear. He looked at the others, starting to have second thoughts.

'She's going to be really angry, isn't she?'

Gwen tried to shrug it off. 'You never know. Maybe you were right, maybe she wants help with something.'

'Maybe,' said Ianto. 'Maybe she's starting a bowling league, and wants us to form a team.'

Jack looked even more worried now. 'I don't think she's starting a bowling league. Doesn't seem the type. Hold on, here she comes… Ah, Detective Swanson! Always a pleasure to hear your voi—'

He yanked the phone away from his ear, wincing at the volume and intensity of Swanson's response. Gwen and Ianto couldn't make out what she was saying, but it didn't sound good, and any time they could make out a word, it wasn't a good one.

Almost a full minute later, the shouting stopped.

Jack grinned, trying on the charm. He couldn't help himself. 'You kiss your mother with that mouth?'

Ianto and Gwen glanced at each other, and shook their heads. Wrong move. Detective Swanson was not, in their experience, someone who responded to charm. This wasn't going to end well.

Jack yanked the phone away from his ear again, as Swanson started shouting at him again. Finally, after what seemed like a lifetime, he managed to get a word in.

'Are you going to tell me what we've done to deserve these sweet nothings?'

He listened again.

'The rest of the team?'

Gwen and Ianto frantically mimed at him to say that they weren't there, shaking their heads and waving their arms around. Jack grinned. Why let them miss out on all the fun?

'Yes. We're all here, hang on.'

He pressed the speaker button, and replaced the handset.

'OK, go ahead, you're on speaker with all three of us.'

Swanson's voice came out of the speaker. 'Oh good. The Three Stooges. What an absolute delight.'

'And what can we do for you this evening, Kathy?'

'Don't presume to be on first-name terms with me, for a start.'

'Sorry. Detective Swanson.'

'Oh, you're going to be sorry. But before that, perhaps you could explain a few things to me, just to satisfy my curiosity. First, what the hell were you playing at on that council estate over the past couple of days? Second, why did you go in and break up a drugs gang without clearing it with me first? And third – and I can't WAIT to hear the explanation for this one – why the hell is there a large, smoking crater where the Happy Price supermarket used to be?'

Jack looked at Ianto and Gwen. They shrugged and waved their arms around, as if to say 'don't look at us, mate'. He tried to think quickly.

'I can't really discuss an ongoing case. It's confidential.'

'Ongoing! Oh, good! So there'll be more death and destruction, will there?'

'No, the matter is… taken care of. It's over. We're just tying up loose ends and writing up our reports. That's all.'

'Really. You'll forgive me if I don't believe you, based on past experiences.'

'Trust me. There was a situation involving a hostile

aggressor, but the threat has been neutralised. And that's all I can really tell you about it. But it's done.'

Swanson sighed. 'Oh, I really hope that's true. Does that mean there's not going to be any more fun and games involving you lot? In the near future, anyway?'

'You have my word. We don't have any other investigations at the moment.'

'Good. I don't want to hear a single, solitary word about any of you for a week. Two weeks. Minimum. It's hard enough doing my job without having to worry about bloody Torchwood creating news stories.'

'News stories?'

'Turn your TV on. And stay out of trouble. Or I'll come down there, and smack you around. And not in a good way.'

Click! She slammed the phone down, making them all wince.

Ianto coughed, and reached for the TV remote. The news story was already under way, with helicopter footage of the ruins of the supermarket.

'... and still, the full scale of the blast is unknown, with police and firefighters unwilling or unable to say who or what is responsible. Early reports that it was caused by a gas leak are still unconfirmed. The only silver lining to this bizarre tale is that nobody appears to be seriously injured.'

Jack, Gwen and Ianto looked at each other, sheepishly. Behind them, on the screen, the scene changed to a reporter interviewing a pair of shocked survivors, covered in dust and silver emergency blankets.

'I'm talking now,' said the reporter, as if he was in a warzone, 'to Nina Rogers and Jessica Montague, who were shopping at the time of the explosion. When did you first become aware that something strange was happening?'

'It was crazy,' said Nina, blinking at the camera light. 'There was this mad woman with this big gun – I think it was a gun, it was definitely some sort of weapon, I don't know – and she was waving it around, screaming at everyone. We didn't see much after that, we just got out of there. I mean, if we had been even a tiny bit slower, we'd have been caught in the explosion. It—'

Ianto turned over to another news channel. Then another. Then another. All featured footage of the aftermath of the explosion, with headlines like 'Gas leak?' and 'Possible gas explosion', but none of them seemed to have anything concrete to say regarding the actual cause, the people involved, or anything at all. There were no developments, but for the rolling news channels it was business as usual – there was very little to say, but they had twenty-four hours of screentime to fill.

Ianto turned the TV off. He looked at the other two. 'Well, at least there's no mention of us.'

'Yes, but it's all over the news!' said Gwen.

Jack shrugged. 'They all seem to think it was a gas leak. The heat-cannon won't leave them any obvious clues, so they'll have to go with that. We got off lucky. Fairly lucky.'

Ianto raised his beer bottle. 'Here's to a better kind of luck next time.' He swigged it, and reached for another.

***

The next morning, Gwen walked into the Hub, yawning. She strolled over to Ianto's area, but was horrified to find that the coffee machine was switched off, and there was no sign of Ianto. Trying to stay calm, she opened her desk drawer, looking for her guilty secret – an emergency stash of instant coffee, hidden under several folders so that Ianto wouldn't find it. Tragically, the jar was empty. She ran into Jack's office.

'Coffee,' she said. It was all she could manage. Jack raised his eyebrows, so she repeated it, but made it into a question. 'Coffee?'

'Oh, Ianto's off getting his supplies. Last Thursday of the month, remember?'

'Is it? Already? Bugger. Just have to wait, then.'

'You could always go and buy a cup from the café around the corner.'

Gwen looked at Jack, dismayed, as if he had suggested she shoot a small kitten in the head. 'Jack, Jack, Jack. He'd go bananas. He'd kill us. And he'd be able to smell it, too, he knows what the coffee from all the local places smells like. He hasn't let us set foot in a Starbucks since…'

Jack winced. 'Yeah, that was… well, kind of funny, really.'

'Not for me, it wasn't. Where does he get it from, anyway? His special stuff?'

Jack shrugged. 'No idea. He won't even tell me. Probably climbs up a mountain, or something. Picking it, bean by bean, just to make sure.'

'Wouldn't surprise me.'

'He should be back in an hour or so, if you can handle

waiting that long.'

'I'll give it a go. Any more fallout from last night?'

'Seems to have calmed down. The gas leak story is sticking, so I think it's a done deal.'

Gwen nodded at him, and went to her desk. Just as she sat down, an alarm went off.

'Oh, what now?'

She looked at the screen. And then grabbed her gun. Jack came running out of his office, gun drawn. 'What is it?'

'Motion sensors,' Gwen shouted. 'There's someone else in here with us, and it's not Ianto.'

'Where?'

Gwen checked the screen, unsure where to aim her gun.

'It's not clear, can't get a fix on it. There!'

She aimed her gun, but there was nothing there. Just a slight shimmering of the air.

'Something's here, but I can't—'

Swish! A tiny dart embedded itself into Gwen's neck. She flinched, and pulled it out quickly. She looked at it, frightened.

'Jack! I've just been shot with a dart, get into cover!'

Jack ran for his office. Swish! Another tiny dart got him on the arm. 'Dammit!' He knocked it off quickly, and came storming back down towards the centre of the Hub. 'Gwen, are you OK?'

'I don't know. Don't feel any different. Where the hell is it…?'

She checked the screen again, but the scanners were still having trouble pinpointing the location.

And that's when they heard the voice.

'Don't bother looking. I'm using a camouflage suit, top-of-the-range Yu-Ca grade from J'rizon 12. Harkness, I know you'll have heard of that.'

Gwen and Jack looked at each other. Jack nodded. 'Yeah, I have. Who are you? What do you want?'

'I'm the father of the child you murdered yesterday. What I want, is for you to die.'

'We didn't murder anyone,' said Jack. 'It was the woman that your parasitic kid latched on to. She'd had enough, didn't want to be its puppet any more. We tried to stop it.'

'Your involvement resulted in the death of my son.'

'There was nothing we could do. If you hadn't abandoned your kid, none of this would have happened.'

'Abandoned? I didn't abandon him, he was taken from me. He was caught in the Rift, along with my mating partner. She was killed, and my son did what he needed to do, to survive. He found a new host. I've been tracking them for a while. And if I had found them, I could have taken my son home, leaving the human female unharmed. Now, thanks to you, I have nothing, apart from a lifetime of pain. And that is what I am giving you, in return.'

Gwen put her hand up to the pinprick in her neck, rubbing it. 'What did you do to us?'

The alien moved around silently, never giving them a chance to focus on its voice for too long.

'I've infected you with the Kagawa Virus. Again, I presume you know what that is.'

Jack looked sick with worry. He tried to hide it from

Gwen, but failed. Gwen knew it must be pretty bad if even Jack was scared – what could possibly frighten a man who couldn't die?

'Jack? What does that mean? What has he done to us?'

Jack looked away, unable to answer.

'Jack? Tell me!'

'He won't tell you, so I will,' said the alien. 'It's an alien synthetic developed from the venom sacs of a Kagawan lizard, which renders its prey unable to fight back. It sends a feedback loop into your mind, which occupies it completely, making you unable to do anything or even move. Slowly, it will render you completely motionless, but aware of what's happening to you, trapped inside yourselves. It's a form of living death. And the only sort of death that will work on someone who can't die.'

'Give us the antidote,' shouted Jack. 'Or I'll find you, and hurt you, I guarantee it.'

'You can't hurt me. You've already taken away everything I had. I never even bought the antidote, I had no intention of letting you use it. Very shortly, you will both go into a sort of waking coma. You, Cooper, you'll eventually die of old age, still in that condition. But you, Harkness – you will just go on, for ever, gradually going insane, unable to die. You can't heal yourself, there isn't actually any physical damage to heal, just the feedback loop going around and around in your mind. You will spend an eternity, suffering, inside the now-useless meat of your body. Already it's starting to take effect, and you're losing your concentration, having trouble thinking clearly. In a few minutes, you'll be unable to stand up or feed yourselves, and will enter a permanent vegetative state. It's what you deserve.'

Jack and Gwen moved towards the sofa, unable to keep themselves steady. Gwen looked at him, scared. 'Jack? I can feel myself going, I can't – I can't focus. Can you stop this?'

'I don't know. I don't think so.'

'But we're one person short,' said the alien. 'Where is Jones? Where is the tea boy?'

'I'm here,' said Ianto suddenly.

BANG! The alien's head exploded in a fountain of blood, and his camouflage suit shorted out, revealing his body, which stayed standing for a moment before crumpling to the floor. Ianto blew the smoke from the end of the shotgun, and removed his night-vision goggles. He glared at the alien. 'And I'm not the tea boy. I'm the coffee boy.'

Ianto raced over to Jack and Gwen, who were already sitting still on the sofa.

'Ianto,' said Jack. 'He said there was no antidote, what are we going to do, I don't have an antidote, I can't fix this, I don't know what to do, I—' He was babbling, partly because of the confusion sown in his mind by the virus, partly out of sheer panic.

Ianto shushed him, and checked his pulse before checking Gwen's. 'He didn't say there was no antidote, he said he didn't buy it. Which means he bought this virus from somewhere. Which means I can find out where, and get the antidote. I'll fix this. I promise. I'm going to take care of things. I always do.'

'Ianto,' said Gwen, trying to concentrate, trying desperately to form the words which might be her last. 'If you can't get it, if you can't cure me – don't let Rhys see me like this. Don't make him spend the rest of his life looking after me. I can't let him go through the pain of watching me slowly die for the next however many years. Don't let that happen, OK? Finish it. You take my gun, and you finish it.'

'Hey!' said Ianto, more sharply than he intended to. He softened his voice. 'Hey. It's not going to come to that. I'm going to take care of things.'

'But if you can't – promise me. Give me that much.'

Ianto took a long look at her. 'If it comes to that, then I'll do what needs to be done. But it won't come to that.'

'Thank you,' said Gwen.

Ianto looked at Jack. Jack just shrugged, and said nothing. He couldn't ask Ianto to kill him, because he couldn't die.

'If you can't fix it,' said Jack, 'just put me somewhere. Freeze me. Won't make a difference to me either way. Don't waste your life on this. On me.'

Ianto put his hand over Jack's mouth to shut him up. 'You're not giving the orders now. And I'll do what I like. So, with all due respect, shut up.'

He removed his hand, and kissed him, quickly, keeping his expression optimistic. He looked at them both, holding on to their hands, gently. 'I'll stay with you until the virus takes over. Then I'll go and sort this out. And then we'll all go and get drunk. Deal?'

Gwen and Jack nodded, unable to speak now, growing ever more still. They were fading fast, slipping into the living death caused by the virus. Ianto held their hands, and waited, smiling, looking as if this was all just a tiny hiccup in their daily routine, something easily fixed.

Jack tried to stay focused on Ianto, his breathing getting slower.

Gwen stared straight ahead. The last thing she saw before the virus took her over completely, was the photo of Tosh and Owen on her desk.

And then, finally, they were both motionless, sitting silently on the sofa. Ianto checked their breathing – slow but steady. They were both now in the waking coma that the alien had promised.

Ianto made sure they were comfortable, and not in any danger of falling or choking. He gave them one last look, his confident expression vanishing, as he crumpled for a moment, wondering what the hell he was going to do.

And then he sprang into action.

Ianto checked the database for more details on the Kagawa Virus, but the files didn't contain any more than the alien had already told them. He paced up and down, trying to think, and talking out loud to himself, occasionally directing comments at the motionless figures of Jack and Gwen.

'OK, so Big Daddy tracks his missing kid, comes through the Rift to Earth, and sees what happened at the Happy Price. He realises his kid's dead, decides it's our fault, and spends the night doing research, finding out who we are, and figuring out how to get inside. So. There's no reason why he'd have the virus with him already, he was just looking for his missing wife and son. Which means…'

He looked over at Gwen, snapping his fingers.

'Good idea, Gwen. He must have bought it *after* he arrived. Which means he got it somewhere locally. He didn't get it from us, we didn't have any samples in the safe. So where would he have picked it up from? Hmm?'

He glanced at Jack, as if hearing something.

'Yes! That's right. We already know that someone has been selling alien tech on the black market recently, under the radar – it must be a local group. Obviously we don't know for certain that Big Daddy got the virus from them, but it's our best bet. So… how do I find them?'

He stared at Jack and Gwen, thinking.

'If they've sold this virus to other people, there'll be reports of the symptoms. People suddenly slipping into comas, waking comas. Well, it's a start. Good work, you two.'

Jack and Gwen didn't move. Ianto sighed. 'Well, if I'm talking to you, then I'm not talking to myself, which makes it perfectly normal and not weird…'

He sat down at a computer, and started searching through police reports, hospital patient records, anything and everything. An hour later, he saw it. It wasn't much, just a tiny reference in a hospital admission, someone falling into a waking coma, with no other symptoms. They were discharged when the doctors couldn't figure out what was wrong with them.

And there was an address.

Ianto hurried along the ninth floor of the block of flats, looking at the directions he'd hastily scribbled on a piece of paper. When he came to number 912, he rang the doorbell. It was opened by a hollow-eyed woman in her thirties.

'Caitlin Hirschman?' asked Ianto.

She nodded. 'Who are you?'

Inside the flat, Ianto and Caitlin sat at the kitchen table, sipping at mugs of tea.

'It was horrible,' she said. 'One day, he was just gone, like he'd been switched off. As if there was nothing inside, you know? But when I looked into his eyes, I could tell he was still in there, he was just trapped, stuck in his own head. At least if his mind had gone, it wouldn't be as bad. But I knew he was feeling it, every moment.'

Ianto nodded. 'When did it happen?'

'Six months ago. I came home, he was on the sofa, I thought he was messing about. But he wasn't. Doctors couldn't find anything, what a waste of bloody time that was. I brought him home in the end. I said, if you can't find anything, or do anything, then at least he can be at home, with someone who loves him, looking after him.'

Ianto glanced through the open kitchen door, to the living room. It was empty.

'Where is he now?'

'He died, a few weeks back.'

'I'm sorry.'

'It was suffocation, they said; must have swallowed his tongue or something.'

She looked away, unable to meet Ianto's eye. He noticed this, but didn't push it.

'Did he know anyone who might have wanted to hurt him?'

Caitlin looked up sharply. 'Why? You said you were with the police. What's this all about?'

Ianto sighed. Time to come clean.

'The same thing has happened to two people who are very important to me. I'm trying to save them. But they didn't just come down with it. It was done to them. It's a manufactured virus that doesn't exist in the wild, and someone infected them with it. If your husband had the same thing, then it would have been deliberate. Somebody did it to him.'

Caitlin stared. 'Somebody did it – deliberately? Why?'

'I don't know. Did he have any enemies? Rivals? Business partners?'

'Business partners, yeah right. He was a schemer, my Joe. He'd buy and sell stuff, cheap crap, you know, the usual. Didn't always go well. He did get warned off once, but we didn't think any more of it. He was trying to sell electronics gear in some industrial estate, but this company told him to stop. It was their patch, apparently. Sounded well dodgy if you ask me. But that's all. They wouldn't have done this though, surely?'

'I don't know. Worth a look. Have you got their address?'

'Yeah, in the spare room. Joe kept everything, all the receipts, travel tickets – drove me mad, I said, what do you need all that for, not like you're doing it for the taxman or anything. He was funny like that, though. Never threw anything away.'

She started to cry softly, and Ianto waited patiently, not

pushing, keeping his voice gentle. 'Why don't you tell me where to find it, and you can wait here and finish your tea?'

In the spare bedroom were several piles of folders, receipts, and boxes filled with all sorts of cheap electronic gadgets. Ianto went to work, finding the piece of paper he needed first, but having a look through the rest of the stuff just in case. He sifted through several boxes of junk, but then found one which was a bit more interesting.

In among the cheap radios and toys, was a small alien device. Ianto picked it up, recognising it, and checked that it was still working. The power was fairly low, but it came on. He pressed the right sequence of buttons, and a rough holographic copy of himself appeared, several feet to his left. He waved at himself, and quickly switched off the device, slipping it into his pocket.

He looked again at the sheet of paper that Caitlin had guided him to. The company name was Conlan & Co. Electronics.

At the front door, Caitlin stopped Ianto before he left.

'Your friends,' she said. 'It's definitely the same thing as my Joe?'

'Looks like it,' said Ianto.

'Well then do yourself a favour. Do *them* a favour. Kill them. Just put them out of their misery.'

Ianto shook his head.

'I'm not doing that, until I've exhausted every other option.'

'Well, when you do… just kill them. Because believe me, they are in absolute agony. My Joe was, I could see it in his eyes.'

Ianto nodded. 'He didn't swallow his tongue, did he Caitlin?'

Caitlin just looked at him. And closed the door.

The industrial estate was filled with empty warehouses, and shuttered buildings covered with 'To Let' signs. Not very promising. Ianto wandered around, trying to get his bearings, wondering if industrial estates had light-bending qualities.

'Unit A3, A3…'

There was a Unit A4, and a Unit A2, but no A3. Apart from a hand-lettered sign: 'A3 relocated to C14'. Ianto sighed and retraced his steps.

Outside Unit C14, Ianto tried to look through a window, but the inside was painted over. Faint cracks of light leaked through – someone was in there. Ianto opened the door, and walked into a large reception area.

It was empty, apart from three sofas, and a small desk with a computer. Ianto coughed.

'Hello? Shop?'

Behind the desk, a doorway led into the main warehouse. Ianto was just about to investigate, when a bored woman in her twenties came through. She shielded the doorway as she came in, so that Ianto couldn't see past her into the warehouse.

'Can I help you?'

181

'Yes. You can. I'm here to buy some of your alien merchandise, please.'

The woman looked at him blankly. There was a flicker of reaction in her eyes, but she kept her face neutral. She glanced down at her computer screen, and turned it off.

'We're export only. Don't do foreign.'

Ianto kept his voice level, but never broke eye contact, watching for her reaction. 'Not foreign. Alien.'

'Is this a joke?'

'I never joke about alien merchandise. I'd like to buy some. So why don't you tell whoever's in charge to come and see me.' He looked up at the security camera in the corner of the room, and took out the small alien device he had taken from the room in Caitlin's flat. 'Just so we're all on the same page – I'm looking for stuff like this.'

He flicked the device on, projecting the holographic image of himself for a few seconds, then turned it off again.

'Like I said. Alien merchandise. I haven't got all day.'

The receptionist stared at him. The intercom crackled, and a voice came through: 'It's OK, Salina, I'll be there in a sec. How about some coffee for me and my guest?'

Salina shrugged, and went to the coffee machine in the corner. Ianto beamed at her, and waited. Eventually, a tall, thin man came through the warehouse door. He smiled at Ianto, as if inspecting a laboratory specimen for dissection.

'Hello. My name is Alix. With an I. How can I help you?'

Salina brought two mugs of coffee over, and put them down. She stood there, waiting. Alix glanced at her. 'Thank you, that'll be all.'

She muttered something to herself, and went back into the warehouse, shutting the door. Alix smiled. Ianto took a sip of the coffee, and winced. To say it wasn't up to his standard would be like saying a light bulb emitted slightly less light and heat than the sun.

'OK, Alix-with-an-I,' said Ianto. 'Let's cut to the chase here. I need to buy the antidote for the Kagawa Virus.'

Alix opened his mouth to protest, but Ianto cut him off, waving a hand dismissively. 'Save the denials, I haven't got time. I know you've been supplying it, I know you used it on Joe Hirschman when he strayed into your territory, I know you've been selling alien equipment and weaponry to various gangs, thugs and other undesirables around the country. But right now, I don't care about any of that. Nobody else knows, and I'm happy to leave it that way. I just need that antidote, and I need it now. Sell it to me, and you'll never see me again, or anyone I work with, and you can carry on with your little business.'

Alix took all that in, and smiled. 'Fine. Seeing as we're cutting to the chase. I know you're Torchwood. I sold the virus to a very angry man, a man who asked a lot of questions about you lot, so I have to assume, seeing as the other Torchwood kids are not here, that he used it on them. I have the antidote. But it'll cost you.'

'How much?'

'Five hundred thousand.'

Ianto blinked. 'Excuse me?'

'It's normally less than that, but I'm acutely aware that you're desperate, so the price is adjusted accordingly. Supply and demand, you see. And I've heard stories about your resources, so I'm fairly confident that you can easily lay your hands on that sort of money. It's enough to reward me for my time, but not so much that it'd raise alarm bells with your people.'

Ianto raised one eyebrow. 'You gave him the virus, knowing he was going to attack us with it?'

'Yes. Because I knew one or more of you would escape, and eventually track us down, and be willing to give us a lot of money for the antidote.'

'We could have all died!'

'I didn't force him to attack you. I merely provided him with a weapon. My responsibility ended there. And look, here you are, alive and well, and with a marvellous, bulging bank account.'

'You knew what the virus could do. And you let him loose with it.'

'Yes, yes, I'm very, very naughty, and I feel simply terrible about it. Does that make you feel better? We can debate this for hours, but the simple fact of the matter is, if you give me five hundred thousand pounds, I'll give you the antidote, and everybody will be happy. I know you can get the money.'

'Of course I can get it. But it'll take a few days.'

'Then you should probably start working on it now. I'll bet if you really try, you can have the money by this evening.'

'That's impossible.'

'Well then consider this. The longer you leave it, the less chance the antidote will work. In twenty-four hours, it will be all but impossible to cure, even with the antidote. So I suggest you stop wasting time talking to me, and run along to your paymasters.'

Ianto stepped forward, face like thunder. But immediately, two large men armed with guns stepped into the room, from inside the warehouse. Alix smiled. 'Don't embarrass us both, Mr Torchwood. I have more friends than you do. And they're not as polite as me. Off you go.'

Ianto glared at Alix. 'If I can't save them—'

'Yes, yes,' said Alix, interrupting. 'You'll kill me, and so on, and so forth. Time is ticking away. Tick tock. Tick tock.'

Ianto left without another word.

'I thought I said I didn't want to hear from you lot ever again,' said Swanson. 'Or at least for two weeks. I thought I was quite clear about that.'

Ianto paced up and down next to the SUV, making faces into the phone. 'I wouldn't call unless it was urgent.'

'It's always urgent. But not for me. As usual, it's just Team Bloody Torchwood getting involved in things that would have stayed perfectly fine if they'd just left well alone. And you want me to send out a unit, without a search warrant, to help you break into a legitimate business property and arrest a load of people without charge, so that you can steal something from them?'

'Well when you put it like that, of course it sounds bad. But they're bad people.'

'Why?'

Ianto hesitated. 'I can't tell you why. You wouldn't believe me.'

'Try me.'

Ianto sighed. Made a decision.

'You know what? There's no point. I'd have to spend a good half an hour here arguing with you, trying to convince you it was real, then I'd have to bring you to our Vaults to prove to you that I'm not insane, and by the time you grudgingly admitted I might be right about certain things, it'd be too late, and you'd still want proof that these people were up to something. And I don't have that proof. I just have my word.'

There was a long pause as Swanson considered all this. But ultimately, she was a member of the police, and there were some lines she just couldn't cross.

'I'm sorry. But your word isn't good enough. Especially if it means possibly ending my career.'

'Fair enough. I'll do it myself.'

'I didn't hear that.'

'I know. But you'll hear all about it by the morning.'

Ianto hung up before Swanson could say anything else.

He was out of options. Apart from the one, really dangerous option that might get him killed. Business as usual, then.

He got into the SUV, started it up, and sped off.

Ianto strode into the Hub, a man on a mission. He glanced over at Jack and Gwen as he passed, and gave them a cheerful wave.

'Only me,' he said. 'Don't get up.'

He went deep into the darkest recesses of the Hub, past

the cells, past the vaults, past all the other storage areas, until he came to the small, tightly locked door labelled 'Weapons'. He spun the submarine-style wheel, and quickly tapped at the keypad, entering the code that he wasn't supposed to know.

Click! The door opened, and he walked into the large, dimly lit warehouse. He knew what he was looking for, and headed straight for one particular compartment. He took out a large, sinister-looking alien device which couldn't have been more obviously a gun if it had had 'THIS IS A GUN' painted on it, in blood. Ianto switched it on. It whirred and hummed alarmingly, sounding like a nuclear reactor firing up.

'Nice.'

He left the warehouse and locked the door again. He moved on to the armoury, and sorted through the various guns and knives, deciding which ones would be the most useful, which ones didn't pack enough of a punch, which ones would slow him down. He packed several of them into a large rucksack, and secreted the rest in his clothing, making sure they didn't stick out too obviously.

He walked back into the main area of the Hub, calling out to Jack as he carefully placed the rucksack and alien gun down.

'Don't feel bad that I worked out the code for the weapons warehouse. You did a fantastic job of keeping it secret, honestly, you really did. Took me ages and ages. It's no reflection on you at all. It's just that I'm very crafty.'

He knelt down in front of Jack and Gwen. He turned to Gwen first.

'I don't know if either of you can hear me, but if I don't make it back from this… Gwen, sometimes you drive me bloody mad, but I wouldn't want it any other way. You're brilliant, and gorgeous, and so brave, and we're lucky to have you.'

He turned to Jack.

'Jack. You know how I feel. I think I know how you feel. You brought me back from the brink, so many times, and made me feel so alive. I didn't think I'd ever feel like that again. So thank you. In all the madness, you're the one person I know I can rely on. And that counts for a hell of a lot.' He hesitated, then grinned. 'Also, you've got a great arse. But you already know that.'

Ianto stood up again and went to a computer screen. 'If anything goes wrong, you'll both be looked after. I mean, in the way you wanted.'

He recorded a video message for Rhys, explaining what had happened, and what to do. Then he recorded another one for Martha Jones at UNIT, telling her what to do with Jack if Ianto didn't make it back. He knew he could rely on her to do what was necessary. Sure, she'd probably spend a few months trying to figure out another way to cure them – and who knows, maybe she'd even succeed – but if it came to it, she'd finish the job as Ianto had asked. He closed the messages, and set up the server to send them in twenty-four hours. If he didn't come back, then at least things would be taken care of.

He turned back to Jack and Gwen.

'Right, then. I'll be off. Do some killing and maiming.

Hopefully I'll see you soon.'

Before he left, he gave Jack one last kiss. And he made sure it was a good one.

He looked at Gwen after kissing Jack. He shrugged, and gave her a long kiss too, one that was almost as good as the one he'd given Jack. He glanced over at Jack. 'What? Not like you don't get to snog everyone. And I think I deserve it.'

He walked to the main exit of the Hub, taking one last look back. And then walked out.

The SUV screeched to a halt outside the warehouse, and Ianto stepped out, bringing his rucksack with him. He strode towards the front door.

Inside the reception area, Salina the bored receptionist was tapping away at her computer when Ianto walked in. He put his rucksack down, which clanked and rattled. He coughed politely. She looked up.

'Hello. Me again. Get Alix-with-an-I to come out and play, would you?'

'Hold on.' She clicked a button on the intercom.

Ianto smiled at her. 'Your coffee's rubbish, by the way.'

She just shrugged.

Ianto continued. 'And your attitude doesn't help. If you don't care about the coffee, why should anyone else? It's lacklustre. Uninspired. When you take a sip, it should get you excited about the day. But yours? It's like licking a damp, smelly towel. One that's been left in a musty cellar. If you're not going to do it properly, don't do it all. Coffee's too important for that. I don't normally talk this much. It's just

189

that you're not really filling in your side of the conversation, not at all, and I just feel compelled to keep talking about nothing. Do you get that a lot? People just rambling on at you?'

She shrugged again.

Ianto nodded. 'Thought so. Your attitude to conversation is the same as your attitude to coffee. Oh, thank God.'

His last sentence was a reaction to Alix walking through the door, finally.

'Hello, Mr Torchwood. That was quick.'

'Not for me, it wasn't. Thought I was going to end up talking myself to death.'

'I meant, you were quick getting the money.' He pointed at the bag.

Ianto smiled. 'Ah, right, I see. Well, it's not like that, exactly.'

He pulled out the massive alien gun and switched it on.

Alix stared at him. 'Mr Torchwood. This really isn't wise.'

'Oh really? Why not?'

'Because I have more toys than you do. And more people.'

'We've already established that. So bring out your two little friends, and let's get this over with.'

'Oh, I've got more than two friends.'

Alix snapped his fingers, and ten large men came through the warehouse door. They surrounded Alix, protecting him and aiming their guns at Ianto. The largest one stood right at the front, in Ianto's line of fire. He looked like he was made of gorilla meat, a huge stack of it, painted to look roughly like a human being. He was actually human but, in Ianto's line of work, he could be forgiven for having to take a second look to make sure.

'Ah,' said Ianto. 'I'd kind of planned on only having to deal with two of them.'

'This is Sean,' said Alix. 'Say hello, Sean.'

'Hello, Mr Suity-Man,' said Sean, chuckling. The other large men chuckled with him.

'Don't make fun of the suit,' said Ianto, shaking his head in disapproval. 'Just don't.'

'So,' said Alix. 'Now that we've established our dominance in this little game of posturing, perhaps you'd be so good as to hand over the money. Then we can give you the antidote, and we can all go on our merry way.'

'Right,' said Ianto. 'That's not going to work for me. You see, I don't have the money.'

'You need more time?'

'No. I didn't even try to get it. I knew it would take too long, and I can't risk wasting any more time.'

'I must have misunderstood. What are you saying? What's in the bag?'

'No money. But a whole load of guns.'

Sean chuckled again, but stopped when nobody else joined in. There was an awkward silence.

'The thing is,' said Ianto, apologetically. 'I know there's quite a lot more of you than I'd expected. But I'm going to have to go into that warehouse behind you. And I'm going to take the antidote from you. Without paying.'

They stared at him for a moment.

Sean burst out laughing. The other large men joined in this time. Ianto laughed too. Even Alix cracked a smile, amused by the situation. There was general hilarity for a good minute or so.

When the laughter gradually died down into occasional snorts, Ianto shrugged at them. 'It's true,' he said, smiling.

Sean stepped forward slightly. 'And how are you going to do that, Mr Suity-Man?'

Ianto stopped smiling. 'Well, I'm going to walk forwards. And I'm going to blow open that door, with this.' He waved the alien gun. 'And if you try and stop me, I'll have to hurt you, probably kill you. You see, I really don't care what happens to any of you. Whether you go to prison, hospital or the morgue. Makes no difference to me. You deliberately set Torchwood up to get infected with that virus, so you could blackmail some money out of us. So right now, all I care about is getting that antidote. And if I have to kill every one of you, then I will. And I won't even look back or think twice about it.'

The mood grew solemn, as the others realised how serious he was.

'Won't look back, eh?' said Sean.

'That's right.'

'Well, you should have looked back a minute ago, when Matt came in through the door and pointed a gun at your head.'

'Really.'

'Yep.'

Matt was a few steps behind Ianto, aiming his gun, just as

Sean said. But Ianto didn't even bother looking. He smiled. 'You expect me to believe he's really there?'

Sean looked uncertain. 'Well… he is.'

'Right. And suppose I shoot you in the head? Will Matt shoot me?'

Sean was acutely aware that the alien gun was pointing right at his head. 'Damn right he will.'

'OK. But – and please do correct me if I'm getting this wrong – you'll be dead before he shoots me, is that right?'

Sean hesitated. He looked over Ianto's shoulder quickly, at Matt.

'Matt, shoot him now—'

But Ianto was already firing the gun over his shoulder. He aimed the gun back at Sean again, before anyone could react. Behind him, he heard the sound of Matt slumping to the floor. Ianto looked surprised.

'Well, what do you know. He really *was* there. And I'd have bet good money that you were bluffing. Now I feel silly.'

'This has become tiresome,' said Alix. 'Take him.'

'OK, wait!' Ianto held his hands up, aiming the alien gun away from the men. 'Look, there's way too many of you, I won't be able to get you all. Let's just talk about this, and work something out.'

'Kick the bag over here first,' said Sean. 'Give us the guns, and that fancy gun thing too.'

Ianto nodded. He slid the rucksack over to them, and threw his gun to Sean, who caught it in one hand. Sean leaned down to open the rucksack. Ianto closed his eyes and blocked his ears.

'Wait!' shouted Alix. 'Don't open—'

BANG! Inside the rucksack, the five flash grenades went off, creating an enormous, bright flash of light and an incredibly loud bang.

Everyone in the room staggered backwards, temporarily blinded and deafened.

Everyone except Ianto. Who opened his eyes, unblocked his ears, and got to work.

He pulled two guns out, and dived to one side, firing at the men, who were now firing blindly all around them, desperately trying to hit him. Some of the men were hit by friendly fire, but most were taken down by Ianto, quickly, coldly, efficiently. He got two immediately, and carefully got the rest, using bodies as a shield, moving around silently, always moving, always getting closer to the warehouse door. The last few men that survived, he gave a choice.

'Drop your guns, and walk out of here. And I won't come after you.'

One of them did, running out, eyes streaming from the flash grenade's after effects. Two stayed, and struggled to reload their guns. Alix disappeared into the warehouse, slamming the door behind him.

Ianto marched up to the remaining two men, and swiftly took them down with a succession of hard kicks and punches. Salina the receptionist popped up from behind the bullet-ridden desk, and ran for him with her own gun, but he ducked, then knocked her out with a roundhouse punch. He looked down at her.

'See? When you put some effort in, it's much better.

Miserable cow.'

He reloaded his weapons, picked up the alien gun, and stepped over to the door.

Inside the warehouse, the door exploded off its hinges and Ianto ran through the smoking doorway. At the other end of the warehouse, Alix was crawling on his knees, still having trouble seeing. He fired his gun over his shoulder, unable to focus on anything. Ianto walked right up to him, getting a bullet in one arm for his trouble. He shot Alix in the leg to slow him down, kicked the gun out of his hand, turned him over, gripped him by the hair, and slammed his head into the concrete.

'Where's the antidote?'

'I'm not going to—'

SLAM! 'Where's the antidote?'

'I'm not telling you—'

SLAM SLAM! 'I can do this for a long time. Where's the antidote?'

'Why don't you—'

SLAM SLAM SLAM! 'How long before your skull cracks? How long before you start bleeding into your brain? How long before you turn into a drooling vegetable? WHERE. IS. THE. ANTIDOTE?'

Alix's eyes glazed over with concussion, and he gave up. 'Crate G21. Same crate as the virus.'

Ianto walked away without another word, and found the crate. He opened it and found several packets with syringes inside. He read the labels, and checked them against his own list that he'd printed off from the Torchwood files. Alix had told him the truth – it was the antidote. While he was at it, he took all the containers of the virus, too, so he could dispose of them safely later.

He walked back over to Alix, who could see a bit better now, but was still concussed. He glared at Ianto.

'You've made the biggest, and last mistake of your life. I'll find you, Mr Torchwood. I'll find you, and your friends, and I will make sure th—'

'Save your breath,' said Ianto, activating a small, purple cylinder and placing it on the ground. The device started beeping. 'This is a Tregennan demolition bomb. Makes big boom-boom. Better start crawling – you've got sixty seconds to get out.'

He held up his stopwatch, and clicked the button. He turned to go.

'You shot me in the leg,' said Alix. 'I can't make it out that quickly.'

'Give it a try,' said Ianto, as he walked towards the exit.

Alix swore under his breath, and started crawling slowly away from the bomb.

Outside, Ianto got into the SUV and phoned Rhys.

'Rhys, it's Ianto. Meet me outside the Hub in thirty minutes. I need your help, it's urgent.'

He hung up before Rhys had a chance to argue or ask questions. Behind him, the warehouse exploded in a massive fireball. The sixty seconds were up. Ianto started the SUV, and drove away.

And, as promised, he didn't even look back or think twice about it.

The SUV came skidding to a halt near the tourist entrance of the Hub. Rhys, who had been waiting nearby, ran over.

'What's going on? Where's Gwen? Bloody hell, are you all right? You're bleeding.'

'It's just a flesh wound. I hope. Gwen's inside, and I'll need your help.'

They ran into the Hub. Rhys saw Gwen and Jack on the sofa.

'Gwen?' He stared at her, then at Jack, realising something wasn't right. 'What's happened?'

Ianto got two antidote syringes out, and walked over to them.

'They've been infected with a virus. It sends a feedback loop into their mind, meaning they can't think about anything or do anything, it's sort of a waking coma.'

'You what??'

'This is the antidote.'

Ianto rammed the syringes into their arms, and pressed the plungers.

'But it doesn't just work by itself. You have to coax them out of it. You need to talk to them while it works through their systems, and remind them of every single strong, positive memory you can think of, anything their mind can latch on to and use to focus itself back.'

'Why didn't you tell me this had happened before now?'

'Rhys, we don't have a lot of time. I've given them the

antidote, now we need to make it work. I'll explain everything after, we can have a great big rollicking Welsh argument, but right now we need to pull them out of it. You take Gwen, I'll take Jack.'

'What do I say? Just, sort of, nice things that happened to us?'

'Yes, anything like that. Stronger the better.'

Rhys knelt down by Gwen, Ianto sat with Jack. They both started talking, Rhys self-consciously, Ianto quickly and efficiently.

'Er, right then,' said Rhys. 'Hello sweetheart. Good memories... God, they're all good, at least, you mainly remember the good ones, don't you? Right, well, where to start? Our first kiss. First date. First time we... you know. Moving in together, we were so scared, but excited, we didn't leave the flat for three whole days. Me mate Steven thought I'd had an accident or something, cause I wasn't in the pub all weekend, he was a right laugh. The day we got married. That was fantastic, it all worked out in the end, even though I was convinced these muppets would mess it all up.' He glanced over at Ianto, awkwardly. 'No offence, like.'

Ianto wasn't listening.

'The day we all had to go to the five-star hotel, to avoid meeting our previous selves,' he said to Jack. 'And the meal we all had that evening. That time in the Hothouse, when Gwen caught us, and you kept doing impressions of her reaction. Naked hide and seek. After we stopped those alien parasites from infecting everyone, when everything turned out OK, how relieved we were – then we all went and got totally rat-arsed. You were dancing on a table, and Tosh was shoving fivers in your belt. Me and Owen said she was paying too much, that you'd do it for a drink and a wink, and I spilt my drink all down Gwen's cleavage. Laughing, just laughing like we'd never laughed before, in case we'd never get another chance.'

They both carried on, digging deep, getting as personal as they could, neither one of them caring about being overheard now. Desperate to save the person they knew, the person they loved.

Suddenly, with a gasp, Gwen snapped out of it. She tried to stand up, but staggered back onto the sofa.

'Easy, easy love,' said Rhys, gently. 'You're OK. You're OK.' He pulled her to him, holding her tightly, kissing her head.

They both looked over at Jack, who was still catatonic. Ianto was still talking, non-stop, trying everything he could think of.

'That time we came into your office, and we'd all switched clothes just to make you laugh. Gwen was in my suit, Tosh was in scrubs, and me and Owen were wearing Gwen and Tosh's clothes. You laughed so hard, the coffee came out of your nose. Then you made me wear...' He glanced over at Gwen and Rhys, slightly self-conscious. 'Made me wear it again the next night.'

Gwen and Rhys smiled, but were concerned now. Jack still wasn't coming out of it. Ianto kept going.

'You getting that bloody clown mask, and sneaking up on us all, for days on end. Me and you dancing at Gwen and Rhys's wedding. The time we saved that kids' party from the

Astracane leeches, and they let us have a go on the bouncy castle. The stopwatch.'

Jack still wasn't responding.

Ianto looked at the other two, panicking. 'He's not coming out, I don't know what else to try.'

'There must be something,' said Gwen.

Ianto stared into space, thinking. And then he thought of something. He smiled, and looked back at Jack.

'How about that time when—'

He stopped, and looked at Gwen and Rhys. He didn't want them to hear this. He leaned in closely to Jack, and whispered the rest into his ear.

And whatever it was, it did the trick. Jack lurched forward, taking a sudden, gasping breath, and jumped to his feet, not realising how weak he still was.

'Oh, MAN that's a relief,' he yelled, before falling forwards onto his face.

They manhandled him back to the sofa, propping him up. Gwen was fully recovered now, and able to stand without support, but Rhys clung on to her anyway, just in case.

'Just relax, your muscles need a few minutes to warm up,' said Ianto. 'You'll be fine. You'll both be fine.'

'Thank you,' said Jack, quietly.

Ianto nodded. 'Just doing my job.'

'So what was it, then?' asked Rhys. 'What pulled him back? We couldn't hear.'

Ianto looked at Jack, who grinned and said, 'A gentleman never kisses and tells.'

Gwen howled with laughter. 'Oh, you bloody do, though!

Come on, give! What was it?'

'Not this time,' said Jack. He mimed zipping his mouth closed. Gwen looked at Ianto, hoping he would answer, but he shook his head.

'Maybe I'll tell you when you're older.'

Later, just before Rhys took Gwen home, Jack bandaged Ianto's wounded arm.

'So could you hear everything?' asked Ianto. 'When I was rambling and trying to figure out what to do?'

'Yeah,' said Jack. 'I remember it all. Including the kiss. Both of the kisses.'

Ianto looked embarrassed. 'Let's keep that between ourselves, eh? I don't think Rhys would appreciate it, even if it was a last goodbye sort of thing.'

'What's it worth to you, for me to keep it quiet?'

Ianto thought about it. 'A few things immediately spring to mind.'

'I bet they do. But if I can remember everything while I was infected, then so can Gwen.'

Ianto stared at him. Then turned back to look at Gwen, who was just leaving. She winked at him, and blew him a kiss. 'No tongue next time,' she yelled, giggling.

'Hey, what does that mean?' asked Rhys, as they walked out.

Ianto sighed. 'You two are never, EVER going to let me forget this, are you?'

'Depends. You'll have to be extra nice to me.'

'I'll consider it.'

Jack grinned, then finished bandaging Ianto's arm. 'So…
if you couldn't save us – would you have frozen me? Got rid
of me?'

Ianto was silent for a moment before answering.

'No. I'd have looked after you. Every day. And I'd have
figured out how to fix you, somehow. Even if it was the last
thing I ever did.'

Jack nodded. Took Ianto's hand.

And for the rest of the evening, there were no more
words.

Consequences

JOSEPH LIDSTER

'OK, I wasn't sure what was the best thing to open with. Because it's kind of about the main girl, but it's more about this Torchwood thing. So, I thought it could start with like a snappy teaser opening. Something like…'

Bigger than the police! Way bigger than the army! Catching aliens and fighting zombies! Putting things right that once went wrong! This is the story of a top-secret Government organisation called Torchwood!

'And then, it cuts to the main character. Cos she's like our… I don't know what you call it. Focus character?'

The blonde woman smiled. 'You mean we're seeing it all from her viewpoint?'

'That's it! Sorry, this is sort of my first book so, erm… Right, anyway, she's standing in Cardiff Airport… And, I'm babbling so, look, I'll just read it, and you can tell me what you think.'

***

Nina Rogers was standing in Cardiff Airport's car park, and she wasn't sure why. She looked up at the grey clouds rumbling across the sky. Then she blinked as rain splashed into her eyes. She shook her head, trying to shake off the now-familiar fuzziness. *How did I get here?*

'Oh, sorry,' she muttered as someone bumped into her. She wasn't sure why she'd apologised as it hadn't been her fault. The problem for Nina was that she hadn't been sure about much recently. Everything was all a bit grey. All the time. She looked over at a gaggle of smokers, huddled under the awning in front of her. They were a thoroughly miserable bunch. Sucking desperately on their cigarettes as they watched the rain splatter around them. One of them looked familiar. A man. In his twenties. Quite fit actually. As Nina watched, he finished his cigarette and flicked it down a nearby drain. Then, he looked up. And he looked at her. And—

he's running towards her. Trying to get through the hospital doors. Trying desperately to get away from something and she's pushing forwards and she can see others behind him but they don't look right. They're shambling towards her and the doors are closing behind the man. Glass doors. She can see them. They're dead. And the pain in her leg is forgotten as she realises what they are and—

She blinked and looked down at her leg. It was fine. It'd healed up ages ago. She looked back up at the man as he gathered up various items of luggage and children and hustled them into the Terminal building. He seemed to have about forty-eight kids, all of whom were in various stages of having a tantrum. One of them, a little girl, dropped a doll. A horrible gothicky thing. As the girl bent down to pick it up, Nina watched as—

a girl and her Gran running down the aisle towards her and they're all running. Running from the hideous black alien blob that's absorbing everything in its path and they're in an office and the Gran is exploding in a mess of—

She blinked as a woman's voice cut through her thoughts.

'I said, are you all right, luv?'

Nina turned to look at the woman. 'What?'

The woman, resplendent in Elizabeth Duke's finest, waved her hand in front of Nina's face. 'It's pissing down. You're getting soaked.'

Nina looked down at the puddles at her feet. The water rippling around her.

And realised, to her genuine surprise, that she was the centre of the universe.

Then she looked up and saw *him*. No, she wasn't the centre of the universe. He was. The man striding towards her. The reason she was here. Again.

And he's on the street, outside the house telling her to find somewhere else to live. And he's in the hospital car park, fighting the zombies. And he's in the toy shop with Jane Austen. And he's saving the world. Always saving the world.

She blinked as she remembered. *Captain Cheese.*

'Can you see him?' Nina turned back to the woman. 'That man. Can you see him?'

207

The woman gave her a funny look and walked off, muttering something about student loans and drugs. Nina wasn't listening though. She was watching the man as he strode towards the car park. He seemed to be talking into the air. And grinning like an idiot.

'OK, Ianto, so you got a bit wet. Just bring the car round.' There was a pause, then he laughed. 'It rains in India as well. We just got lucky.' He jumped, looking startled. 'And tell Gwen I heard that! That woman's got a filthy mouth.'

Laughing, he strode right past Nina and towards the car park. Towards the now-familiar black SUV that was pulling up at the exit. He gave the car's occupants a wave, then, suddenly, he turned around and looked right at Nina. His silvery-blue eyes were like car headlights slicing through the rain, and she found herself stepping back.

'Hey there,' he grinned. 'We've got to stop meeting like this.'

Nina Rogers blinked once. Then she ran.

'So, you've named the main character after yourself?' asked the blonde woman, still smiling. 'That's… interesting.'

Nina Rogers looked up. 'Sorry?'

The woman, whose name Nina had already forgotten, reached across the desk and touched the open manuscript. Nina looked down at it.

'Oh, yeah. Well it's kind of based on real events.'

The blonde woman nodded, looking thoughtful. 'Well, it's got a good opening. Nice and mysterious. But I'd need to hear more, if we're going to consider publishing it.'

Nina blinked, confused for a second. Then she looked down at the manuscript.

'That was the introduction so now it carries on with the title and then into the proper story and—' She cut off and grinned for the first time since she'd arrived at the publisher's office. 'Sorry, I'm babbling again. I do that when I'm nervous. Motormouth, my mum calls me. And now I'm babbling about me babbling and—'

The other woman put her hand on Nina's arm and smiled reassuringly. Nina fell silent and took a deep breath. Then she began.

'It's just, this story. It needs telling. I have to tell my story.'

TORCHWOOD

CONSEQUENCES

Nina Rogers

You spin my head right round... right round...

Nina Rogers was curled up, eyes closed, and she was singing to herself. Hearing footsteps approach, she stopped singing and opened her eyes. Two smart shoes were striding towards her face.

'Morning,' she croaked, lifting her head and looking up at the owner of the shoes.

Rianne Kilkenny just frowned, stepped over Nina, and clicked on the kettle. Which was when Nina realised she was on the kitchen floor. Again.

'Oh,' she said, obviously bemused.

'Late night, was it?'

Nina, using the oven to support herself, staggered to her feet. 'Yeah,' she answered weakly. 'Guess it was.'

Rianne turned away from her and grabbed two mugs off the draining board. Silently, she popped a teabag in each one and stared at the kettle.

Nina cleared her throat. 'You OK?'

Rianne nodded.

There was a pause. Then Rianne turned to face her.

'OK, I wasn't going to say anything, but I've got to, OK?'

Nina leant back against the oven, surprised at her mate's outburst.

'You're drinking too much.' Rianne paused. Then it all came out. 'I know it's not my place to tell you how to live your life but, come on, Nina, it's every day now. Every day since you moved in, I've come downstairs and I've found you passed out. It's not good for you.'

She paused for breath, but Nina interrupted her before the lecture could continue.

'Well, I'm sorry, *Nurse* Rianne, but it's not like you're not on the wine every night. If you want me to move out, just say so.' Instantly, she felt guilty for snapping. No, not guilty. Confused. It just wasn't like her.

There was a pause before Rianne replied. She was clearly trying to stay calm. 'I said you could stay here as long as you liked, and I meant it. I'm just worried about you.' She turned away from Nina, then continued. 'Where were you last night? Can you remember?'

Nina shrugged. 'Yeah. I was out with Jess. We were…'

She trailed off as Rianne, still with her back to her, sighed and shook her head. 'Jess came round last night. She was looking for you because you weren't answering your phone.'

'I…' Nina didn't know what to say. 'But… I must have been out with…'

As Nina tried to remember, Rianne poured water into

the mugs. She went to the fridge and got the milk. Then, unable to find a clean teaspoon, she gingerly pulled the teabags out of the mugs. She handed one to Nina, who took it without speaking. They stood there, in silence.

Then Rianne spoke. 'Still can't remember?'

Nina stared into her tea. Watching it ripple as she blew on it. 'I... I dunno. It must have been someone else. I can't remember.'

Rianne smiled sympathetically. 'Look, it's OK. We all get bladdered once in a while. But this is every night.'

Nina nodded, lost in thought. She was desperately trying to remember what had happened. She'd had no tutorials in the afternoon so she'd gone to the library. Then she'd gone... She thought about the various pubs and bars in Cardiff. Picturing them in her mind. Trying to force herself to remember which one she'd been in. Bar Reunion... Terra Nova... the Priory... Tiger, Tiger... Exit... None of them rang a bell. And she wasn't sure she cared. She just wanted her head to stop spinning.

Rianne looked at her watch, then put her mug down. 'Got to get to the hospital. I'm going to be late.'

She strode through to the hallway and grabbed her coat. 'Remember, two of my ladies are due today, so I'll probably be late back.' She opened the front door then stopped. She came back to the kitchen and put a hand on Nina's arm. 'Just have a night off, yeah?'

Nina nodded and smiled at her friend. Then, as a plane flew over the house, she jumped, splashing her tea down Rianne's uniform.

Rianne swore and rushed over to the sink. She grabbed a cloth and started scrubbing herself down. 'No, it's OK! No need to say sorry or anything!'

But Nina could feel herself drifting away. Rianne was becoming a blur, and all Nina could see were aeroplanes flying over her head and rain splashing into her eyes. She struggled to focus, staring down at her mug of tea. *Oh God, not again.* The tea was rippling. The puddles were rippling. Rianne was asking if she was OK. Elizabeth Duke Woman was asking if she was OK.

'Nina? I said, *are you all right, luv?*'

Nina desperately tried to look at her friend but everything was so grey and unfocused. Then she heard another voice. And, gradually, she realised it was her own.

'*Nina Rogers was standing in Cardiff Airport's car park and she wasn't sure why.*'

She was vaguely aware that, miles away, in a kitchen somewhere, Rianne Kilkenny was coming towards her. 'What are you doing?'

'*She looked up at the grey clouds rumbling across the sky. Then she blinked as rain splashed into her eyes.*'

'Nina? Stop taking the piss.'

But Nina ignored her. She heard her own voice continue.

'*She shook her head, trying to shake off the now-familiar fuzziness.*'

Somehow she was aware that her flatmate was storming off down the hallway, but it was only when she heard the front door slam that Nina blinked and her vision cleared.

She looked around the empty kitchen, confused. Then she shrugged and sipped at her tea. 'I've really got to have a night in,' she muttered.

Nina Rogers was standing in the Millennium Centre's café and she was still waiting for her coffee. Her mate Jess, standing next to her, had taken a break from having a go at the desperately slow waitress to have a go at Nina.

'Oh, come on! Just one night out. One little night out!'

Jessica Montague was officially a Bad Influence, and Nina told her so. They paid for the coffees and went to sit outside.

'And why the hell have we come here?' asked Jess. 'We'll have to get a bus to Uni, and I hate buses.'

Sitting down, they both looked around the Bay. As Nina put her bag down and wrapped the strap under the leg of her chair, she found herself staring across at the water tower.

'I wonder where the water goes,' she muttered.

'What?' asked Jess, already ripping open a third sachet of sugar. 'What water? Where?'

Nina nodded over towards the metallic structure in the centre of Roald Dahl Plass. Water cascaded down it and into the ground at the base of the tower.

Jess laughed and shook her head. 'Who cares! Now come on, please. Night out? Just one. Please. Even Jean's up for it!'

Nina turned back to face Jess. 'Oh, I don't know. I really need a night off.'

Her friend frowned and, muttering something, determinedly stirred her coffee.

'What?' asked Nina. 'And careful! You're making a right mess.'

Jess's stirring had sent coffee splashing onto the table. Nina watched as the breeze blew ripples across it.

Puddle. Rippling at her feet. Tea. Rippling in her mug. Coffee. Rippling—

She forced herself to focus on Jess. 'You OK?'

'It's just that, I dunno. You seem to be out every night at the moment, but it's never with me. God, I don't want to sound like a needy bitch but you're meant to be my mate. I had to go out with Tess last night. Tess!'

'Things that bad?' Nina smiled. 'Oh, I'm sorry. OK, OK, we'll go out tonight. On one condition.'

Jess took a sip of her coffee, leaned back and lit a cigarette. 'What?'

'We go to the library. Today. And we work our arses off.'

'Nina!'

'I mean it! We've fallen well behind this year already.'

'Can you blame us?' Jess shook her head, laughing. 'After everything that's happened, really can you blame us? First, there were those bombs! Then there was that serial killer—'

Nina laughed. 'Yeah. He went after people who could sing, Jess. You were never in any danger.'

'Bitch!' Jess grinned. 'My "Pokerface" is still talked about. But yeah, come on, we had that mad bugger then...' She trailed off. And they both stopped smiling.

'It was a gas leak,' Nina muttered, remembering *that* night. The night the city had been overrun by the living dead. So many had died and, still today, people weren't sure what had happened. There was talk it might have been terrorism or even aliens, but terrorists used bombs and aliens came in spaceships. And they kept coming. Over and over again.

'And then there was the Happy Price,' continued Jess. 'We could have—'

'Oh God, let's get pissed tonight,' announced Nina, desperate to forget. 'Let's just get really, really pissed.'

Jess smirked and reached down into her handbag. She sat back up, brandishing a hip flask. 'Why wait till then? Splishy-splashy?'

Nina laughed as Jess poured some whisky into their coffees. Then she looked over at the water tower and she stopped laughing.

A man was standing next to it. Him. Why was he following her? Why was she following him? Captain Cheese gave her a wave...

She quickly bent down, untangled her bag from the chair and stood up.

'Come on. Library. Work then play.'

And, ignoring the WTF expression on Jess's face, Nina Rogers strode off.

'This man, "Captain Cheese".' The blonde woman smirked then continued. 'Do you know his real name?'

Nina looked up from the manuscript, slightly irritated

at the interruption. She shook her head. 'Well, I didn't back then. But I'm trying to tell this in some kind of order.'

The other woman nodded and smiled. 'That's fine. I was just wondering when you first met him.'

'I… I guess it was…' Nina tried to shake off the grey fuzziness. 'Well, I think I saw him at the hospital when the… you know… the zombies invaded.'

'OK, well, carry on.'

Nina sighed as the bus stopped yet again. 'Why are there so many stops? If people weren't so bloody lazy…'

She trailed off as she became aware that Jess wasn't—

'No, wait!' Nina stopped reading and looked up. 'I had seen him before, I remember.'

'When was that, then?'

'It was before the Daleks invaded. I was in a club. One in the Bay that's closed now. Which isn't surprising cos the music was shite. But I was at the bar with some mates when he came running past. There was a guy in some kind of monster costume and he was chasing him.' She paused, confused. 'I'd forgotten about that.'

The blonde woman nodded, clearly trying to look sympathetic. 'Seems like there's a few things you've forgotten.'

Nina took a sip of water from the glass the woman had given her when she'd arrived. 'I'll just… I'm just going to carry on reading.'

***

Nina sighed as the bus stopped yet again. 'Why are there so many stops? If people weren't so bloody lazy...'

She trailed off as she became aware that Jess wasn't listening. Her mate was busy applying lip balm, flicking through a copy of *Heat* and having her own little rant.

'I mean, was he expecting me to call him? After that? No bloody way. I don't care how bloody fantastic his thighs are, I don't do being stood up.'

Nina nodded and smiled. She'd long ago realised that Jess rarely required a vocal response.

'Rhodri Lloyd is dead to me. Because of him, I had to go out with Tess!'

Nina grinned over at her friend. 'I thought that was my fault.'

'Oh yeah, I'm blaming you as well. But this is me, Jess Montague, Officially Giving Up On Men.'

Nina laughed and turned to look out of the window. Then, she stopped laughing. Because through the glass she could see a man. A man holding a sign reading 'Horoscopes – this way. Only £5!' And she remembered—

The man on the telly was calling for them. He was calling them by their star signs, and he was making them walk. She was trying to stop Jean when the American ran past her.

'Let her go!' he said. 'Just get indoors, and lock yourself in.'

Then he continued running, calling for Ianto. Ianto...

Nina Rogers was sitting in Cardiff University's Library and she was trying not to look like she was staring at the Fit Bloke. She was meant to be reading the book that lay open in front of her but she was kind of finding it hard to care about the Ottoman Empire. Especially when she could Definitely Not Stare at *him*. Dressed immaculately, he obviously wasn't a student. She'd always liked a bloke in a suit, and this one filled his out nicely. He was standing, looking a little lost, in the History section. Fiddling with his cuff-links, he seemed to be waiting for something to happen.

And Nina knew that something would happen. Because it wasn't just that she fancied him. She knew him.

She's standing at the bar, watching him chase the monster through the nightclub... And she's looking out of the hospital window, watching him and Captain Cheese fight off the zombies... And she's standing in WH Smith's, and she's watching as he rugby-tackles the orange man with the glowing copper ball... And he's looking up at her and grinning and she's grinning back and—

'Put your tongue away!'

She jumped as Jess appeared behind her. 'Honestly, Nina, why don't you make it a bit more obvious and get your tits out?'

Nina tried to smile. Tried to pretend that everything was normal. 'He's fit, though, isn't he?'

Jess shrugged and sat down next to her. 'If you like the lost little Welsh boy look.' She yawned dramatically. 'OK, I've been and I've looked at the books. There's lots of lovely books in here and I'm sure they're all fascinating, but we could be in the pub.'

Nina grinned. Even when she knew the world was wrong. Even with the suited man standing just a few paces away, Jess could somehow make everything seem normal.

'No!' She wagged a finger at her friend. 'No pub. Not until we've done some work.'

Jess put her head in her hands. 'I'm so bored. And there's no decent totty in here.'

'I thought you were Officially Off Men?'

Jess laughed into her hands. 'Yeah, right.'

'You are so pathetic.' Nina reached over and pulled Jess's hands away from her face. 'Rhodri Lloyd stands you up and you're Officially Off Men for all of an hour and...' Nina trailed off. Jess was looking at her blankly. 'Jess?'

'Who's Rhodri Lloyd?'

Nina felt the world lurch. She gripped Jess's hands, then flinched, recognising the expression on her friend's face. It was the same one she saw in the mirror every morning.

'You said he was dead to you.'

Jess giggled. 'Are you pissed?'

'Less than an hour ago. On the bus. You were talking about him. He was meant to be taking you out last night. You were *just* telling me about him!'

Jess shook her head. 'I've really no idea what you're on about.'

Nina's grip on Jess's hands tightened. 'You saw him last week in Exit. Said he looked like Sam Warburton. He was meant to be taking you to Abalone's.'

223

'As if I'd go there. It's a dive.' Jess laughed then pulled her hands free. 'I swear you're losing it.'

Nina Rogers just looked at her friend. And she knew that the world was wrong. And she tried to fight it but she could feel the panic rising. The same panic she'd felt in the hospital and the toy shop and the supermarket and WH Smith's and all those other times she'd witnessed Hell on Earth and she knew that there was nothing she could do. She felt her eyes welling up with tears as she stared at an uncomprehending Jess. Jess Montague, the one normal thing in her life. Jess who'd just forgotten the bloke she'd been talking about all week.

'Nina?'

'I think… I think you're right. Oh God. I am losing it.'

Jess's face blurred as the tears came. And Nina Rogers started to sob. She didn't care where she was. She wasn't even sure she knew where she was. She only knew one thing. And that was that there was something wrong with her. And that it wasn't going to go away. The universe hated her and the world was broken. Hot tears poured down her face. 'I just want it to stop!'

'Handkerchief?'

Nina blinked and looked up.

The suited man had crouched down between her and Jess. He was holding up a pristine white handkerchief.

She took it, apologising. 'I'm not normally like this. I'm sorry.'

'It's OK.' The man smiled. 'I'm Ianto Jones and I'm here to help.'

And, for just a moment, the world stopped spinning.

Nina Rogers was crouched on the floor at the back of Cardiff Library. Her old friend, Jessica Montague, and her new friend, Ianto Jones, were sitting on either side of her, and they were listening as she told them her story.

'I'll skip a bit now as I've already told you about the airport and the zombies and that.'

The blonde woman poured them both some more water and nodded.

'So yeah. I told them how I kept finding myself in places and how I kept seeing him. This Ianto Jones and his mate.'

'And what did he say?'

'So when did it all start?'

Nina looked over at Ianto and shook her head. 'I don't know,' she muttered. 'I don't even know what *it* is.'

They were crouched between shelves of old dusty books in a rarely used part of the library. Nina turned to Jess who was sipping whisky from her hip-flask. 'You're quiet. Don't you believe me?'

Jess laughed coldly. 'Yeah, I'm not stupid. I've seen the aliens, Nina, of course I believe you. I just can't believe you didn't tell me.'

Nina reached out to hug her but Jess pulled away. 'I'm sorry. I didn't know what it was. I still don't. I just keep finding myself... at places with him.' She nodded over to Ianto who looked uncomfortable, his legs squashed up into his chest.

'It's not me,' he told her. 'It's Jack you're following.'

'Captain Cheese?'

Ianto suddenly let out a huge laugh, surprising Nina. 'Oh, he'll love that.'

Nina grinned over at him. Quiet, studious but with a sense of humour. Yeah, she could see this working. Jess wasn't smiling though.

'Who are you?' She jumped to her feet and looked down at Ianto. At both of them. 'What's Torchwood? And what's happened to me?'

Nina looked up at her. 'It's like how I keep forgetting things. You've forgotten Rhodri.'

'I haven't forgotten him. There's been no Rhodri.'

Nina took out her mobile. Flicking through photos, she found the one she was looking for and held it up.

Clearly irritated, Jess took the phone. Then: 'Oh, hello! He's lovely!'

'That's Rhodri.'

'Yeah, like I'd forget *that*.'

'He stood you up.'

'Maybe he had a reason. I'm sure there was a good reason. Have you got his number?'

'Jess! He was with his girlfriend when we met him.'

'Well, clearly they're not happy together. That's not my fault.'

'We went through this before. How would you like it if—'

Suddenly, Ianto stood up and took the phone. He closed it and grinned at them both. 'Maybe another time, ladies?'

Nina blushed. 'Yeah. Sorry. So... is it me? Has something happened to me?'

Ianto looked as if he wanted to put a hand on her shoulder but couldn't. He straightened his tie and looked past her. 'I don't know. You've been forgetting things, and now so has she.'

'After she told me. She forgot after she told me.'

Ianto nodded. 'When did she last talk about the lovely Rhodri?'

Jess stepped in between them. 'I am here, you know. Hello.' There was a pause, then she stood aside. 'When did I last talk about him?'

'On the bus. On the way here.'

'So she came here and then she forgot him.'

Nina nodded but... 'Wait, isn't that a bit of a coincidence? Are you saying something happened here? On the day we meet you?'

Ianto shrugged. 'Whose idea was it to come here?'

Jess yelped. 'Nina's! It was Nina's idea to come here!'

'I am here, you know.' Nina sighed. 'Yeah. It was my idea to come here.'

There was a pause.

'Is anyone else really confused?' asked Jess.

Ianto reached into his pocket and pulled out what looked like a fancy mobile phone. He started to scan the shelves, and they all listened as the phone thing beeped quietly. He turned to face them and raised an eyebrow. 'You not going to ask me what this is, then?'

The two girls shrugged. 'Boys and their toys,' said Jess,

227

offering Nina a swig of whisky.

They all listened as the machine beeped. In the distance they could hear people turning pages, making notes, studying, quietly flirting but there, at the back of the library, it was silence. Except for the monotonous beeping, and—

'Can we have some quiet in the library, please.'

All three of them jumped as one of the librarians, an elderly woman who clearly hadn't smiled for forty years, appeared around the corner. Nina and Jess were both amused to see Ianto blush. Fumbling, he put the phone thing back in his pocket and apologised profusely.

'What are you doing back here, anyway? Nobody uses this section.' The librarian tutted. 'The books aren't on the curriculum, apparently.'

Before Ianto could speak, Nina piped up. 'Doctor Manning asked me to get something for him. He reckoned it'd be back here. Said it was rare or something.'

The librarian nodded and turned to leave. Then she stopped and stared at Nina. 'Doctor Manning?'

'Head of History? Tall guy. Beard. Likes a...' She mimed swigging out of a glass.

The librarian shook her head, clearly confused. 'So they finally pensioned off Doctor Challis, did they? Poor woman...' Murmuring to herself, she left them to it.

Nina turned to Ianto and frowned. 'Doctor Challis left years ago. She'd know that.'

'Perhaps she just forgot...' suggested Ianto, but Nina knew he didn't believe it either.

'What are we going to do?' she asked.

228

'I should call the others in,' Ianto replied. 'Get the library shut down. Investigate properly and—'

Suddenly, the lights went out.

For a second there was darkness, then a siren sounded as emergency lights lit the room in a sinister green. The siren continued as Nina and Ianto turned to look at Jess. She was standing under a fire alarm, smoking a cigarette.

'I did this once before when I came here with some bloke. Good way to get some privacy.' She shrugged. 'We'd better hide, though.'

Jess Montague was in the library and, before Ianto could move, she'd reached over and pulled him between two sets of shelves. She pressed herself against him, feeling his chest against her. She watched as Nina hid under a desk, then she grinned and looked up at Ianto.

'You're pretty fit under that suit, aren't you?' she whispered.

She laughed as he blushed.

'Oh, don't be so soft. I don't do boyos.'

'I'm not a—'

She reached up and put a finger to his lips as a security guard strode past them. Jess could feel her heart racing. She'd no idea what was going on but this was a hell of a lot more fun than revising. She turned to check that the security guard hadn't seen Nina when—

'Sorry, can you just stop a minute?'

Nina looked up at the blonde woman. 'What?'

229

The woman frowned. 'Well, it's just I thought you… I thought Nina was our main character. You've suddenly cut to Jess's point ofview.'

Nina grabbed the glass of water, mostly to stop her hands shaking. 'It… it had happened again.'

'What had?'

'The thing. You know!'

The woman shook her head. 'I don't know, Nina. You tell me.'

Nina took a deep breath. 'The book,' she whispered.

Ianto gingerly took the book off the shelf. It was bound in old, peeling leather and it looked ancient. Oh, and it had stopped glowing. Nina looked over at Jess who was staring at them, blankly. 'You all right?'

'What happened?' Jess shook her head. 'One minute I'm smoking and the alarm's going off and the next… What's that?' She pointed over at the book Ianto was now scanning.

'It's apparently… mostly safe,' he replied before putting the scanner away. He opened the book. 'Oh.'

Nina looked down at the page. 'Oh.' She looked over at Jess. 'Erm… It's about you. Well, this bit is.' She started to read:

'*Jess Montague was in the library and, before Ianto could move, she'd reached over and pulled him between two sets of shelves. She pressed herself against him, feeling his chest against her.*'

Jess looked down at the book, and Nina felt for her. Her

best mate was clearly freaked out.

'After the security guard had passed,' explained Ianto. 'we came back out from where we were hiding. You were just standing there when...'

Nina took her friend's hand. 'This... beam of light. It was like a torch. It shot out of the book, out of its pages and it just... zapped you.'

She watched as Jess struggled to understand. She was clearly determined not to cry, but Nina could feel her hands trembling.

Ianto turned back to a previous page. He started to read.

'*Jess Montague was standing at the bar and she was like seriously well out of it.*' He smirked. 'Not exactly Shakespeare.' He continued to read. '*She looked over at the fit bloke who was dancing with his mates and she decided that she was going to have him. She needed to do something what with Nina being in one of her Boring Sober Moods. She liked Nina, she really did, but sometimes she found her mate so—*'

He stopped reading as Jess quickly reached over and closed the book. For once, she had nothing to say.

'It's all right,' said Nina.

'Did you come to this section earlier?' asked Ianto, gently.

Jess nodded. 'I... I think so. I was just... Well, I was just walking about so I could tell Nina I'd done some work.'

'It must have taken your memories of Rhodri then,' explained Ianto.

'I'm sorry,' said Nina. 'It was my idea to come here...'
She trailed off as Jess stared at her.

There was an uncomfortable pause. Ianto cleared his
throat. 'So, this book takes your memories and turns them
into a story. Right. I suppose I've seen stranger things.'

Nina stared down at it. It looked like an ordinary book.
Old. A bit tatty. There was nothing wrong with it but it was
wrong. She could feel it reaching out to her. Pages rustling
in her mind. Then she let out a cry as—

*—surged up and out of Gran, pouring through the air
vent, the sofa, and streaming in wild tentacles through the
little old lady's ruptured body. At precisely the same time
the outer walls of the office gave in, pouring bricks and
concrete and steel and dust down into the tiny room—*

She fell back against the shelves, terrified. Suddenly the
library seemed so small. So oppressive. Old dusty books
surrounding her, threatening to smother her. 'Why me?'

Jess laughed bitterly. 'It's my memories it's taken!'

Nina shook her head. 'But it's me, isn't it? It's me who
keeps turning up and seeing things I shouldn't see. You
weren't there, Jess! Look! Look in the book and read it.
Read about what I've seen. Read about what I saw in the
toy shop!'

She stopped, feeling the hysteria subside as Ianto took
her hand.

'Whatever it is,' he said. 'It stops now.'

Nina wanted to cry. And she wanted to run. But she

232

looked up at him. 'Why me?'

'You wanted us to come here,' said Jess, quietly. 'You brought me here so it could take my memories.'

Nina just shook her head. 'I don't understand. Is it why I keep seeing the aliens? Is it why I keep meeting Torchwood? Is it... controlling me?'

Ianto was about to reply when suddenly the book started to glow. The three of them jumped back and looked down at it.

'What's it doing?' whispered Jess.

'What it always does,' replied Nina, suddenly remembering so many nights alone in the library. 'Run!'

But before they could move, the book seemed to explode with light. Particles of dust glowed and danced as a shard of light shot across towards them and lit up Jess's face. It pinned her to the wall. Nina tried to pull her free as Ianto ran over to the book. He was pressing a finger against his ear.

'Jack, come in. I need back-up. We need to get this back to the—'

He cut off as, suddenly, Jess started to scream. Nina grabbed her arm and pulled, desperate to free her from the book's beam of light. Jess didn't move. She just screamed and screamed and then she stopped. The beam of light faded away and the book stopped glowing.

There was silence.

'Jess?' whispered Nina.

And Jess turned to face her. For a second, she looked confused. Then she laughed.

'What are we doing here? I thought we were meeting down at the Bay. You know, coffee? It was your idea! God, I even brought my whisky to liven things up a bit and... Oh, hello!' She'd seen Ianto. 'Now don't tell me you're a student here. I think I'd have noticed *you* before.'

Nina put her hands on Jess's shoulders. She looked into her friend's eyes. 'Don't you remember? Please, Jess. This is Ianto.'

Jess shook her head and reached for her hip flask. She held it up then stopped. 'Have you been at this? I only filled it up this morning. It's all right, I don't mind or anything but—'

'What the hell are you lot doing in here? Didn't you hear the alarm?'

They turned around. Standing behind Ianto were three firemen. Nina was about to speak when—

'Oh, hello Mister Firemen,' purred Jess. 'Are you here to rescue us?'

Nina Rogers was standing in Roald Dahl Plass, looking up at the water tower. Despite the breeze coming across the Bay, she still felt stifled. She didn't think she'd ever forget how suffocated she'd felt inside the library. She tried to block out the memory of Jess screaming, and she looked up at Ianto Jones standing next to her.

'You sure she'll be OK?' asked Nina.

Ianto nodded. 'I think it's that fireman we should be worried about.'

Nina smiled. 'Yeah. You should have seen her at Fresher's

Week...' Then she looked down at the book in Ianto's hands. 'What is it?'

'Let's find out.' Ianto walked right up to the water tower and turned back to face her. 'Welcome to Torchwood, Nina Rogers.'

Nina Rogers was standing on an invisible lift as it descended into a secret underground base. She wasn't as surprised as she thought she should be, but she was taking the opportunity to hold on to Ianto's arm. Jess had taught her well.

'You're very quiet,' he commented. 'Normally people gasp at this point.'

She smiled weakly at him. 'After everything I've seen... It's just...'

'You're doing fine, you know.'

She shook her head. 'Am I? I mean, how many memories has it taken from me? What have I forgotten? *Who* have I forgotten?'

There was a pause, but Ianto didn't have an answer.

'Am I even real?'

He turned to face her. 'Of course you are.'

'How do I know? How do I know that book didn't just... make me? Don't you see?'

The lift reached the floor and he led her off it.

Nina stood there, looking around at the madness. 'I don't know who I am any more.'

'That's life, though,' said Ianto. 'I mean, I used to have a girlfriend.'

235

Before Nina could reply, an arm appeared between them. She looked up as Captain Cheese grinned down at her. Then the Captain pulled Ianto into a hug and gave him a tender kiss.

Nina felt like crying. But she didn't. 'Oh, bloody typical. You're gay. Great. No, that's just brilliant, that is. There was me thinking that the one thing, the one good thing that might come out of all of this was a few drinks, a night out, maybe even a quick...'

She trailed off as the two men grinned at her.

'Yeah,' said Ianto. 'I think you're still human.'

Nina Rogers was sitting in a boardroom. A boardroom in a secret underground base. And she was listening as Captain Jack Harkness told her who she was.

'Nina Melanie Rogers. Born on the 13th of July 1988. Lived in Chester with mum and dad until three years ago. Now in your final year of a History degree at Cardiff University. You like Franz Ferdinand, clubbing and the works of Jane Austen. Now, there was a woman...'

Nina tried to hide how unnerved she felt. She looked over at Ianto, who gave her a reassuring smile. 'It's OK,' he mouthed.

'You've had four boyfriends, two one-night stands and what you sweetly call an "experience" with a girl last year when you drank absinthe. You're basically Little Miss Normal except—'

'Except,' interrupted Nina. 'Some old book has taken me over and it's somehow making me follow you.'

'Yeah,' grinned Jack. 'People don't normally need "a book" as an excuse to follow me.'

'Well, not everyone can have good taste.'

For a second Nina wondered if she'd gone too far, but then Jack laughed.

'Oh, I like you. It's a shame you're studying History. I'm thinking about recruiting, but when you've lived as long as I have, the last thing we need is a historian.'

'What?' Nina's eyes flashed with anger. 'What makes you think I'd want to join your little gang? I don't want this. I don't want to be part of it.'

Jack sat down and looked at her. 'Really? You know about all that's out there, and you don't want to see more? You don't want to know about what we do?'

She shook her head. 'I've seen people die. I'm 21. I shouldn't have to see that. I just want my life to be normal.' Her head started to ache as she felt like crying. Again. 'Please, just stop this. Do whatever you have to do and let me be normal again.'

'What's "normal"?' he asked, smirking.

'Normal is not wanting to cry every ten minutes because you don't understand anything any more. You've read all about me, yeah? I used to be a laugh. I used to be strong. I used to enjoy life. That book has taken all that away from me!'

Jack nodded. 'Life has a way of throwing curveballs at you. Trust me, I know what it's like when events... change you.'

Ianto nodded. 'We all do.'

'Well, kids,' announced Jack. 'Let's make Nina normal again.'

'So you wanted it all to be over?' asked the woman.

Nina nodded.

'So why are you here? Why have you written this?'

Nina looked around the office. It suddenly seemed cold. Unfinished. Unreal. The woman wasn't smiling any more.

Nina Rogers was looking at the book. She was in the main area of the secret underground base and she was looking at the book that was slowly destroying her life.

'I want to burn it,' she muttered.

Jack laughed. 'Oh, I think we can do better than that.'

'Don't you want to know what it is?' asked Ianto. 'Don't you want to know what happened to you?'

Nina shook her head. A voice in her head was screaming 'no'. She kept on shaking her head. *No, no, no.*

'Yes,' she said, forcing the word out. Then she gasped. 'Yes, I do.'

'Looks like the real Nina Rogers is still in there,' said Jack with a smile. Then he pulled on a pair of white cotton gloves and opened the book. 'Let's start at the beginning.'

'*Nina Rogers is in the library and she's terrified. There are bombs exploding across the city and—*'

He stopped reading, glancing over at Ianto. 'Well, I think we know what night that was.'

Ianto nodded, and Nina followed his gaze over to a photo stuck to a work console. A man and a woman grinned back at them. Nina wanted to ask who they were. But then she realised that it was the voice in her head that wanted to know. She knew that sometimes you shouldn't ask questions. She forced herself to look back at Jack, who carried on reading.

'*There are bombs exploding across the city, and one of them is so close. The floor's shaking and books are flying off the shelves. One has landed in front of her as she crouches under a table.*

It's me.

I'm the book.

And my pages are blank.

I need stories.

I need stories.

I need stories.

She's reaching down and she's picking me up. She's opening me, staring at my blank pages. A tear, caused by her terror at the bombing outside, is falling/has fallen/will fall onto me and I can taste her. I can feel her. I am her.

I want stories.'

He stopped reading. 'There you go. It's a book. And what do books want?'

'But why me?'

Jack opened the book at a random page.

'*Terry Collins is in Tesco. He's wondering whether he left the oven on. He doesn't think he did. After all, he never used it this morning but he did use it last night and perhaps he left it on then. Perhaps it would take all night for the gas to build up. He doesn't know but he's trying not to think*

239

about it.'

He tried another page.

'Jane Ramsey is humming a tune, and it's really bugging her because she can't remember where it came from. Was it an advert? If so, what was it advertising? It could be sofas or cheese. Something like that.'

And another...

'Moira Raynor is in the library and she's looking over at Doctor Manning. He comes in here every day but he never notices her. She can't blame him. She's old. She knows that. She just wishes he knew what effect he had on her. Just seeing him makes her smile...'

And another...

'Nina Rogers is back in the library. And she's back near me. But she's not thinking about the book or the bombs. She's thinking about last night. She's in the club and she can see two men and a woman chasing a man in a monster costume. At least she thinks it's a costume. People are panicking around them but she wants to know who they are. And one of them is shouting. A barman is asking who he is and he says that he's part of...

'Torchwood.'

Jack looked over at Nina. 'So the book was activated and it wanted stories. And the stories it got were the dull obsessions of ordinary people. And then you came back. And you'd seen us.'

'Nina Rogers is part of me now. She will be my author. I will be her author. She will find Torchwood and she will tell me their stories. She doesn't understand this, but then

there's so much she doesn't understand.

'Nina Rogers is climbing out from under the table, and she's about to put me back on the shelf when she notices the piece of paper stuck inside the back cover. She takes it out and reads it before returning it to its rightful place.'

Jack closed the book and shook it. A piece of paper fell out, and Nina bent down and picked it up. *'Hi Emily,'* she read. 'Emily?'

Ianto shrugged, but Jack's eyes widened. 'It couldn't be...'

'I'm guessing the year is 1899,' Nina continued reading. *'And you're wondering what this is? Well, don't worry about it. Just take it to University College library and put it on a shelf. Don't tell anyone about it. Not Charles or Alice and most definitely not me. That would really screw up the timelines. See you when you get back, love Jack. PS: You would love what the women are wearing in 2009.'*

Nina was staring at Jack and so, she realised, was Ianto.

'It was you?'

Jack took the piece of paper from Nina. 'It's my handwriting.'

Nina sat down, exhausted. 'Why?'

'I remember Emily acting funny back then. When we were dealing with Finch's experiments on...' He trailed off, clearly remembering times past.

'But why would you send it back in time?' asked Ianto.

'I don't know,' Jack shrugged. 'But we'll have to do it again. We've got no choice. If we don't, then we change history.'

Nina and Ianto just looked at him. There was a pause. Then he grinned.

'Oh, screw history. Let's burn it.'

'So that's what we tried to do.'

'You tried to burn it?'

'At first, yeah,' Nina smiled as she remembered. 'We made a bonfire and threw it on, but that didn't work. It just didn't burn. So we took it up to this greenhouse thing they had and tried to feed it to a man-eating plant. It wasn't interested. So we went right down into the depths of their base and tried to feed it to this man-eating alien fish thing they had in a giant aquarium. It wasn't interested. So we took it into this shooting range they had. You know, like the police have in movies. We tried shooting it. Well, they did. I don't like guns. Bullets just bounced off it. They tried to—'

'Sorry,' the woman interrupted her. 'So you're basically saying it was indestructible.

Nina nodded.

Nina Rogers was sitting in Captain Jack's office with two sweaty men. For some reason, they were both grinning. She was glad they were finding it so funny, and she told them so.

'I'm sorry,' Jack replied. 'But we've had all sorts down here, and now we're being beaten by a book.'

'I was always good with books,' said Ianto. 'I was on the Gold colour reading scheme long before the other kids.'

'Oh, I bet you were popular,' replied Jack, grinning. 'You... nerd.'

'Are you two getting off on this?' asked Nina, smiling despite herself.

'Jack gets off on anything.'

The three of them stared at the book that was now wrapped safely in a Quality Mart carrier bag. Despite their smiles, Nina knew, deep down, what was going to happen.

'You're going to send it back to the past, aren't you?'

Jack nodded. 'I'm not sure what else we can do. If we keep it, we can't stop it controlling you. We can't destroy it. All we can do is trap it in a time loop.'

Nina nodded, surprised at how easily she was getting all this. 'So it goes back in time. Your mate Emily puts it in the library. Then over a hundred years later, I find it and it all starts again.'

'But it stops. For you, it stops now.' Ianto stood up. 'That's the main thing.'

He opened the office door that led out to the main area. 'I'll start monitoring for Rift activity.'

He left the office, and Nina looked over at the book then across at Jack.

'What is it?'

'It's a book.'

Nina didn't scream with frustration. She kept her voice calm. 'Yeah, but where's it from?'

Jack stood up and looked out at Ianto. 'Who knows. There are things out there you can't imagine. Stars and planets and creatures that you couldn't even comprehend.'

Nina stood up and joined him. 'But it must have come from somewhere.'

'Yeah, I guess. Or perhaps it's just one of those mysteries that the universe likes to throw at us from time to time.' He smiled, watching Ianto through the glass. 'Like love. And death. And Nando's.'

'And what's going to happen to me? When it's gone?'

Jack turned to face her. 'Honestly, I don't know. You'll either get all your memories back or...'

'Or I'll still be like this. Confused.'

'You know, I don't think you've changed as much as you think. The book's mostly taken your memories of meeting us. You're still Nina Rogers. You still talk too much. There's just a few things that'll seem more like dreams than reality.'

'Like Torchwood?'

Jack laughed. 'Oh, we're real.'

Nina grinned. 'Yeah, I guess you are. And very... gay. It's just the two of you, yeah? Rattling around in this big underground base?'

Jack opened the office door. 'Oh no, we've got Gwen as well. But she mostly just comes in to do the washing up. Like the good little lady she is.'

Nina kicked him.

Suddenly, Ianto called through to them. 'Rift activity!'

Jack ran through the open door, Nina following. Ianto turned to them with a frown.

'You won't believe where...' he said, pointing at the screen.

Nina tried to look but Jack pushed in front of her. She watched as his face fell.

'Oh, not there. Not again.'

Nina Rogers was standing and looking up at the ruined apartment complex.

'SkyPoint,' muttered Jack, standing next to her.

'The most cursed building in Cardiff,' muttered Ianto.

The three of them looked up at what remained of the block. Originally built and promoted as Cardiff's most luxurious living space it was now, after a series of unfortunate events, little more than a shell.

'You bring me to all the nice places,' said Nina quietly as they watched seagulls soar through the upper levels. 'Guess we should go in?'

So the three of them entered what remained of the reception area, Ianto waving his scanner about.

'This way,' he said, leading them up a set of stairs that were covered in... well, even the voice inside Nina's head didn't want to know what they were covered in. The three of them climbed the stairs to the first floor.

'Mind your step,' Jack told Nina as he narrowly avoided putting his foot through a hole in the floor. Ianto led the way, the beeping from his scanner becoming more urgent. He pushed open a door into what once must have been a stunning apartment. Now it was little more than four brick walls with holes where the windows should have been. They headed through to what Nina guessed had been the bathroom and then...

Nina had never seen anything like it. A pool of orange light was floating in the air. It was wrong. It was alien.

'It's beautiful,' said Nina, stepping closer towards it. She could feel her skin tingling and she wanted to reach out and—

Jack grabbed her arm, pulling her back. 'Yeah, it looks good, but it's dangerous.' He grinned. 'A bit like me.'

'You are so full of yourself,' she replied with a smirk.

'Er, when you two are finished?' Ianto sounded irritated. 'The Rift energy's starting to fade, so now might be a good time to get rid of the book.'

Jack handed Nina the carrier bag. 'Do you want to do the honours?'

She took the bag from him and had one last look at the book. She felt nothing. She just wanted rid of it. She lifted the bag and—

'Wait!' Jack shouted. 'Just wait a minute!'

He took the bag back from her and reached in for the book.

'Jack?' Ianto looked scared. 'What are you doing? We've only got a few seconds before—'

'Get me a piece of paper,' Jack interrupted. 'Quickly!'

Nina watched, confused, as Ianto reached into his jacket pocket and pulled out a small notebook. He tore out a sheet and handed it to Jack. Jack quickly crouched down and, taking the note from the book and a pen from his pocket, began to write.

'What are you doing?' asked Nina.

'Trying not to completely destroy the universe,' Jack

246

muttered. 'If we throw the book back with my old note then where's my old note come from?'

Nina's head was hurting and, judging by the look on his face, so was Ianto's.

'Done,' announced Jack, standing up. Then he grinned. 'Look...'

He held up the new note and Nina could tell it was identical. The piece of paper from Ianto's notebook was exactly the same as the note from the book. Jack put the new note in the book and scrunched up the other, putting it in his pocket. He put the book back into the carrier bag and handed it to Nina.

Nina raised her arm, swinging the bag behind her. Then she said two words to the book (which I won't repeat here) and slung it into the orange light. The book hovered in the air, trapped like a fly in amber. And suddenly the pool of light started to expand as it fizzled urgently around the book. Two forces that Nina knew she'd never understand fought for supremacy. She and Jack watched, enraptured by the light show.

'Erm... Jack? Nina?'

She was vaguely aware of Ianto's voice behind her.

'Just want to remind you both that we're in a building that's on its last legs. And we've just thrown an alien storybook into some Rift energy.'

A tendril of Rift energy shot out towards Nina, and she jumped back. She looked back at Ianto, who was heading towards the doorway.

'You ever heard the word "boom"?' he asked.

Nina didn't need telling twice. And neither did Jack.

The three of them started to run.

They ran through the building, dodging bits of falling masonry. Metal creaked dangerously around them and the air was thick with dust. They kept running, down the stairs and into the reception area. Then they ran outside and stopped, breathing in the fresh air. They looked up at SkyPoint, watching as golden light suddenly shot out through the first-floor window panes. And then the building started to crumble so they ran again.

From a safe distance, they watched as the building became dust and Nina knew that the book was gone.

I'm flying through the rift in space and time. I'm flying and I'm crying. Nina's tear is drying and fading and my words are disappearing as the waves of time wash me clean. I'm forgetting everything… I'm forgetting… The aliens and the zombies… Torchwood… I'm forgetting Nina Rogers…

I'm forgetting everything…

I'm forgetting…

I've forgotten…

And the golden light is gone. And it's cold.

I can feel rain. It's splashing me and I don't like it. I want it to stop.

What's that smell?

Roses…

I reach out… Trying to find someone… Something… Anything… Anyone…

Two shoes coming towards me. Hands lifting me. A woman. Her mind tells me she's called Emily Holroyd. She opens me and a note falls out.

'Dear Lord,' she whispers. 'I...'

She says nothing more, but I can see a word in her mind.

'Torchwood'.

I want to know more about them.

I want to know their stories...

Nina Rogers was avoiding the emergency services. Jack and Ianto had told her that would be easier than trying to explain what had happened to SkyPoint. Luckily, there'd been so little of the building left that its final demise had had little effect on the surrounding area. Nina was walking away from it. And away from Torchwood.

'How are you feeling?' Ianto had asked.

She'd told him that she felt fine. Better than fine. She tried to find a nice way to describe it. Something beautiful and romantic. But she'd never been good with words, so the only way she could describe it was that it was the same as having a night off from the drink. That morning where you woke up refreshed rather than lurching into consciousness desperate for water.

She felt alive.

Jack had said they could still help her if she needed it. That they had a special magic pill that would clear recent events from her mind. She'd said no. She'd had enough of alien things in her head. She just wanted to go home.

249

See Rianne. Check up on Jess. She'd had enough of Torchwood.

Then she'd kissed Ianto on the cheek and given him her number in case he ever decided to go straight. He'd laughed, linked arms with Jack and strode off.

And Nina, feeling alive, was going home.

The End

'Except, it's not the end, is it?' asked the woman.

Nina's head felt muggy as she closed the manuscript. 'No…'

'You wanted it to all be over, but here you are, telling me what happened.'

'I have to tell my story…' Then Nina looked up at the woman. 'Why? Why do I have to?'

The woman reached over and took her hands. 'It's OK, Nina…'

Nina blinked back tears. 'I thought it was all over… We got rid of the book but… it's still in me. It's still in my head.' Then she looked up. 'Help me, Gwen.'

The blonde woman smiled. 'You worked out who I am, then?'

Nina smiled back, despite the pain. 'I saw you, just briefly, at the hospital, and I heard you outside Jackson Leaves.'

'And Jack mentioned my name,' replied Gwen, letting go of Nina's hands and taking off her wig. 'Sorry, I needed you to tell me the full story. You needed to get it out of your system while we…'

She trailed off, looking down at Nina's glass of water.

'That drug Jack offered me,' said Nina, quietly. She tapped the glass, watching the water ripple.

Gwen nodded. 'It'll stop the book's residual effect on you.' She stood up and moved around the desk. She sat down next to Nina and put her arms around her. 'Ssh… You're going to be OK. We all are.'

Nina looked up. 'What do you mean?'

'You're going to forget us. You're going to forget Torchwood. But you'll know… Deep down, whatever happens, whatever aliens or monsters come here… you'll know that we exist. Torchwood isn't just a story. We're real. And we're here to protect you.'

Nina nodded because she believed Gwen. Her eyes were closing. She felt so tired. She was vaguely aware of the door opening and two men entering. They looked familiar. She turned back to the woman who told her she was with friends.

And she let herself be led out of the office by the three… people… She was outside now. It was warm. Sun in the sky. She smiled as her eyes closed. And the last thing she saw was three pairs of feet walking away from her.

Nina Rogers was waking up in the street and she was confused. As if she'd just forgotten something.

'I really need to have a night off the booze,' she muttered, standing up. Her mum would be mortified if she ever found out her precious little girl had passed out in the street. The funny thing was, she thought to herself as she started the walk home, she didn't feel hung over. In fact, she felt great. Better than great. She felt… alive. And for some reason, she found herself grinning.

'Sorry,' she said as she bumped into a man walking in the other direction.

'It's all right,' he said, smiling back at her. Nina felt her heart skip a beat. The man was fit. And she'd always liked a bloke in a suit. She wondered whether to chase after him but decided against it. She had revision to do, and Rianne was cooking lasagne tonight.

As she reached the corner, something made her stop. She turned back and saw that the man had stopped as well.

He smiled and gave her a wave.

Then, straightening his tie, the man in the suit turned away from her and was gone.

Acknowledgements

Our thanks go to:

John Barrowman, Eve Myles, Burn Gorman, Naoko Mori and Gareth David-Lloyd, for giving us such wonderful toys to play with.

Julie Gardner, Richard Stokes, Peter Bennett and the rest of the production team, for making it all happen.

All the writers, especially Helen Raynor and Phil Ford (hope you'll join us next time), and Chris Chibnall, for allowing us to resurrect some of his creations.

Mark Morris, Guy Adams, James Goss and Trevor Baxendale, for helping bring Nina to life. And Mark, again, for contributing Rianne Kilkenny to Torchwood's world.

Gary Russell and Brian Minchin at BBC Wales and Albert DePetrillo, Nicholas Payne and Caroline Newbury at BBC Books for constant advice and support.

And, of course, Russell T Davies for… so many things.

About the Authors

David Llewellyn is the author of the fifth novel in BBC Books' *Torchwood* series, *Trace Memory*, and has written the short stories *The Book of Jahi* and *Mrs Acres* for the official *Torchwood* magazine. His other published fiction includes *Eleven*, *Everything Is Sinister* and *Doctor Who: The Taking of Chelsea 426*.

Sarah Pinborough, writer of Supernatural Mystery, Horror, Thriller and Crime fiction, is the author of *Torchwood: Into the Silence*. Her first novel, *The Hidden*, was published in 2004, and she has since written *The Reckoning*, *Breeding Ground*, *The Taken* and *Tower Hill*, alongside many short stories. *A Matter of Blood*, the first book in a new trilogy, will be published next year.

Andrew Cartmel was Script Editor on *Doctor Who* from 1987 to 1989. He has written a novella, an audio adventure and several novels and comic strips featuring the Seventh Doctor, plus fiction based on *The Prisoner* and characters from the *2000AD* comic. His first play was staged in 2003, and his memoir of his time on *Doctor Who* came out in 2005.

James Moran co-wrote *Day Three*, the third episode of *Torchwood: Children of Earth*, with Russell T Davies, having previously scripted *Sleeper* for Series Two of *Torchwood* and *The Fires of Pompeii* for Series Four of *Doctor Who*. He wrote the screenplay for the movie *Severance* along with episodes for several television drama series, including *Primeval*, *Crusoe*, *Spooks* and *Spooks: Code 9*.

Joseph Lidster is the author of the *Torchwood* Series Two epsiode *A Day in the Death*, the first *Torchwood* radio play, *Lost Souls*, a *Torchwood* audio original, *In the Shadows,* and a short story for the official *Torchwood* magazine's 2008 *Yearbook*. As well as contributing stories to the second and third series of *The Sarah Jane Adventures* for BBC Television, he has written numerous audio adventures and short stories for Big Finish's *Doctor Who*, *Sapphire and Steel*, *The Tomorrow People* and *Bernice Summerfield* ranges.